FALL ON ME

By

Penelope Potts

To my husband, Terry – you are always the reason; my four children who make me smile every day; my mum, my sister, Jacqui, and Auntie Mo, who all make me believe that I can achieve anything and that nothing is ever impossible.

Finally, to my editor, Helen Aline Ball, who took on a novel by someone with no understanding of the use of English grammar and punctuation and had never written more than a shopping list, and turned it into something special.

CONTENTS

ABOUT THE AUTHOR

I live in a seaside town in Devon with my husband and four children. I'm a qualified chef and work full-time in a catering business.

My dream was always to unleash my passion to write romantic fiction when I retire, driving around Cornwall in a little camper van with my husband.

One day, the penny dropped: what was I waiting for? Was I really prepared to wait twenty years to release that passion smouldering inside, just waiting for it to ignite?

The following day, I picked up an A4 notebook while doing my weekly shop in Tesco; six weeks later, I had written Fall On Me.

Writing it was amazing; I looked forward to any opportunity to open that notebook and write, almost as if I was the reader, and the words just fell on to the page.

I do hope that you will enjoy reading it as much as I enjoyed writing it. Maybe I will go get myself another notebook!

Chapter One

The black cab turned into Albert Street, lined both sides with beautiful Georgian houses which had mostly been renovated into luxury apartments. Cars parked bumper to bumper the whole stretch of the street.

The driver turned his head.

"Number forty-three, that's halfway up – can I drop you here, love?"

Hollie smiled back.

"Next to that white car will be perfect, thank you. How much do I owe you?"

He glanced down at his running meter.

"Twelve pounds please, miss."

Hollie took the notes out from her purse and passed them over to the driver.

"Thank you, keep the change."

He touched his cap to acknowledge his tip, then got out to open the passenger door.

Hollie had stopped the taxi a short walk from her apartment block so as to enjoy the last few minutes of her evening, making every moment last a little longer. She walked slowly along the pavement, daydreaming of a different ending to her day. Maybe going home to loving parents waiting up for their daughter to return home from a night out, maybe a caring boyfriend staying up to remind her of his love for her. For Hollie was returning to neither of these pleasurable welcomes. Hollie's best friend, Beth, had just turned twenty-one and the girls had been out to celebrate with an Italian meal at Gino's followed by drinks at Billy Joe's, a local cocktail bar. Hollie and Beth had met just three years ago at the start of their veterinary degree at university. Although the girls were practically opposite to one another, Hollie from a fishing village in Cornwall and Beth a glamorous, excitable city girl, the pair soon became the best of friends.

"Just one more cocktail before we go, Hollie, then we'll get a taxi home. I can't get too sozzled as Mum and Dad are putting on a birthday lunch for me tomorrow. Mum hasn't told me yet, but I'm expecting all the family – no doubt Uncle Mac and Aunt Peg will be there. I don't think I can face it with a sore head. It's such a shame you can't make it. Mum loves

2

having you over. I think it is because you're the only one who insists on helping her with the washing up."

"I'm sorry too, Beth – two of the other waitresses have asked for the weekend off so Bob is short staffed and needs me. You know I would have loved to come if I didn't have to work."

The waiter came over to them with two blue cocktail glasses on a tray, with fruit on little sticks and colourful umbrellas hanging out of the top.

"How is that gorgeous man of yours? God only knows how you captured him. I only went to the bar and he came straight over to introduce himself to you. Did he get that promotion in his law firm that he wanted?"

"Yeah, Marcus started last week. He's been given a pay rise with it; only downside is he wants me to give up my waitress job at the diner. He says we don't need the money and my studies are more important."

Beth smiled.

"Poor you! I wish I had a man who would provide for me, so I didn't have to go out to work Why the glum face?"

"You know why. I love my job. I've worked there since we started university. I've made lots of good friends. I know the pay and hours are rubbish, and Bob often makes us work through our breaks, but I love it. I just don't think Marcus likes me working there. He is so protective of me, but in an awkward way. He always insists on coming to pick me up, although he always makes us walk, he never brings the car. It's only a fifteen-minute walk back to the apartment but sometimes it's pouring with rain and yet still he prefers us to walk. Of course, I never complain as I don't want to give him a reason for me to stop working at there."

"Ah, that is kind of sweet, Hollie. I wish I had a fellow who would collect me from places and walk me home."

Hollie looked at her best friend but couldn't quite manage a sincere smile in return. There was a missing piece of the puzzle between her and Marcus. Would she ever find it and make their relationship complete? Hollie's friends and family adored Marcus. He was handsome, well-mannered and had a prosperous career ahead of him. The couple had already moved in together and Hollie's family were awaiting the next chapter in their relationship.

"Happy birthday, Beth!"

The two girls clinked glasses together.

"How did that date go last Saturday night, the one with your brother's friend – Pascal wasn't it?"

Hollie was already laughing as she knew Pascal's English was poor; despite Beth being a chatty person,

4

she would have struggled to have kept the conversation going all evening.

"Well, not exactly what I had imagined. He took me to the cinema, only the film was in Spanish with English subtitles. That wasn't too bad once I got the hang of it. After, we went for pizza but when we were chatting, if he didn't know the English word for something, he would replace it with Spanish. Lovely bloke, but I really should have taken an interpreter."

"Oh, I'm so sorry – if only you had taken Spanish at school, things could have been quite different."

"Don't worry, we didn't exchange phone numbers when we said goodbye. He gave me a peck on both cheeks, muttered something in Spanish, then walked off."

Hollie laughed, biting off the fruit hanging from a stick in her cocktail glass.

"I think I'll go through a lot of toads before I find my Prince Charming. You hardly have to try, Hollie; you just flutter those big, long lashes over those brown eyes and the boys just seemed to come running."

"Don't be silly Beth, I've had plenty of toads in my time."

"Yes, but you have Marcus now. I don't think anyone will cross him to flirt with you – he looks so tough and menacing when another man even just smiles at you, never mind tries to talk to you. Was he really a junior kickboxing champion?"

"Apparently so, before I met him – he's got the trophy at home. Of course, he told me he had to give it all up when he started full-time work."

"Do you remember, not long after you had met Marcus, we went out on a double date to that fancy Italian restaurant? Do you remember we went to the theatre afterwards?"

Hollie closed her eyes, placing her hands over her face, not wanting to be reminded or the horrible occasion.

"Halfway through dessert, a charming fellow that you had gone on a date with, not even a steady boyfriend, briefly came over to just say hello on his way to the bathroom. Marcus was so jealous, he couldn't bear another man that you had dated before him talking to you, even though he was just saying hello. Marcus shouted at him to clear off, and when he didn't, he punched him. The look on his poor girlfriend's face, sitting alone at the table, watching him stagger back to her was awful. We paid the bill and left prompt. Marcus said he didn't like the way he was looking at you. But none of us thought he was out of order. He really has a strange protective manor over you."

Hollie made the corners of her lips rise to form a

smile, but it didn't come from within. Marcus had a nasty protective controlling trait about him. They had only been together for a year – what future could they have together?

"Come on, let's go, we should get a taxi from across the road."

The two girls went outside. The cool evening air was now a little chilly. The taxis were queuing in the layby opposite the cocktail bar. They got into the back of the front taxi.

"Thanks for tonight, Hollie; I've really missed our nights out. We mustn't leave it so long next time. Mum will be shocked when she hears me come home before midnight. Maybe we're just getting old."

The black taxi drove through the city streets for ten minutes before stopping at the end of a driveway to a large, detached house. Beth opened the taxi door.

"Give me a ring soon, Hollie, and don't leave it too long."

"You go steady up that driveway. Send my love to your mum and dad."

Hollie watched Beth walk up the driveway towards her house as the taxi pulled away then headed towards Albert Road. It was only a short drive and just a few minutes later she was walking to her apartment block. She keyed in the code to release the main front door.

On this occasion, she decided not to take the lift, but instead took the stairs. They lived on the top floor, three stories up. Hollie was always careful to be courteous to her neighbours and walked quietly along the corridor. She had two other neighbours on the third floor; one apartment had been empty for some time while the other belonged to Mrs Stuckey. Mrs Stuckey at number eight hadn't long lost her husband and Hollie knew that she would probably still be awake, sitting quietly in her kitchen. Hollie had been knocking on the door more often just recently to see if there was anything she needed – she shopped regularly to get her groceries and often brought back a meal from the restaurant for her, especially if the chef had over-produced a dish that wasn't selling. Yesterday, Bob had given her a plate of lasagne to take home which she gave to Mrs Stuckey. Hollie had knocked several times before pushing the door open.

"Mrs Stuckey," she had called out walking in. "It's Hollie from next door."

"I'm in the kitchen, my dear. Come through."

Hollie went straight up the hallway and into the kitchen. Mrs Stuckey sat on one of the four chairs around a small kitchen table.

"I brought you some lasagne for your tea, Mrs Stuckey. How are you today?"

Hollie glanced around the kitchen, trying not to

8

stare for too long at the mess that it had become.

"What a kind thought. Please sit down, my dear. Would you like a cup of tea?"

Hollie felt warm and comfortable in the old lady's home. Even though it was an absolute mess, it was more homely than her own home with Marcus which was one of the reasons why she loved to visit as often as she could.

"You sit there, Mrs Stuckey, and let me make the tea." Hollie took off her cardigan, slung it on the chair and filled the kettle with water.

"While I'm waiting for that kettle to boil, I'm just going to wash up these few things in the sink. What do you have there, Mrs Stuckey? Is that a photo album?" The old lady sat turning the pages of a large blue album.

"Yes, my dear, so many fond memories all contained in such a small book. I was just looking at a picture of my grandchildren when they were young. Of course, they are all in their twenties now. About the same age as you, Hollie."

Hollie stopped washing up and stepped closer to the table to have a closer look. Four children stood together in a porch at the front of a large house with a pretty garden surrounded by climbing shrubs and roses.

"This house belonged to Mr Stuckey and me many years ago. We sold it to move here, to be closer to our family who had moved to the city. We gave up our friends, our lovely house and garden to be closer to them. Only we didn't consider that their lives had become so busy with their own children and careers that we didn't get to see them very much at all. Now Mr Stuckey has gone, I'm left with only my photographs and my good memories."

Mr Stuckey looked up at Hollie taking her hand. She smiled.

"Don't get old, my dear, not until you have lived and loved your life."

Hollie had smiled at the old lady with heartfelt affection. Although she was lonely, Hollie knew that her heart was full of love and her head full of fabulous memories of the life she had led. Before they had finished drinking their tea, she had finished cleaning the whole kitchen. She put the tea towels into the washing machine, went across the hallway to the bathroom, emptied out the laundry basket, threw it into the washing machine then switched it on.

Hollie looked at her watch. Marcus would be home soon so she needed to get back and start tea. She reached for her cardigan.

"Don't forget to have that lasagne for your tea."

Mrs Stuckey looked up at Hollie. "You're a good

girl. Don't worry about me, I'll be fine."

Hollie took hold of her hand.

"Ring me if you need anything. I'll pop in again soon." Hollie had pulled the front door closed.

That night, Hollie continued to walk quietly up the corridor till she got to her apartment. She unlocked the door and walked straight in. There was silence. Maybe Marcus had gone to bed. She took off her shoes and hung up her coat quietly, then went into the kitchen to get a glass of water to take to bed. Marcus was standing in the kitchen.

"Did you have a good night?" he began. "It looks like you did."

Hollie wanted to give the right answers but there weren't any.

"Yes, Beth and I had a great night, just the two of us, a meal, couple of drinks then taxi home – it was nice to catch up with her." Hollie took a glass from the cupboard and filled it with water from the tap. "I thought you might have been asleep. Don't you have an early breakfast meeting?"

"You know I do, but I couldn't go to bed until I knew you were home. You look like you've had too much to drink."

Hollie took a large gulp of water; she had only had a couple of drinks, so she knew Marcus was just looking for an argument.

"I'm off to bed, Marcus."

She walked into the bedroom, got ready for bed, then set her alarm for the morning. Moments later, Marcus appeared, holding a washing up bowl. Without warning, he took a step closer, tipping the contents over Hollie. Cold water poured over her head, running down her body, soaking her nightwear. She froze for a moment. No words came from her mouth, not even a scream of shock.

"That will sober you up," Marcus said, raising his voice. He then returned the bowl to the kitchen, came back to the bedroom and got into bed. Hollie sat for just a few moments longer, then got to her feet and went into the bathroom to change. Once in bed, her long wet hair soon soaked through her night clothes, causing her to feel cold. She lay completely still. Tears fell from her cheeks, adding to the wetness of the pillow. Her crying was silent, something that she'd mastered recently. The silence in the room was only disturbed by Marcus's loud breathing as he fell into a deep sleep soon after his head had touched the pillow.

Chapter Two

Hollie woke the next morning to sunlight streaming in through the blinds. She turned her head to look at the clock. It was 8 o'clock. She sat up remembering the feeling of being cold from the night before. She was alone in the bed. Marcus had left an hour earlier to go to work. Beside the alarm clock was a glass of fresh orange juice that Marcus must have left there.

Hollie sat up and drank the juice. She knew that Marcus would have been feeling bad for his actions last night and it would be typical for him to be particularly pleasant to her this evening. She knew this because this wasn't the first outburst he had had; there had been several incidents, the aftermath always following the same pattern. He would calm down, and the next evening try his best to make it up to her by telling her repeatedly that he was sorry and loved her. This she truly knew, deep down, could never be possible, as anyone who loved another being with all their heart could never be so cruel to someone they loved. After constant outbursts of anger, it had begun to finally sink in that Marcus couldn't be the one. She knew that sometime soon she would have to find a way to walk away.

Hollie knew that when she returned from work today Marcus would have flowers and a nice meal waiting, his way of redeeming himself. She wondered if he had ever really fallen in love with her or if it was just that her profile and the way that she behaved and looked fitted his lifestyle.

She got up and dressed – she had to be at work in an hour. In under thirty minutes, she was rushing out of the front door, slipping on her work shoes and doing up the last few buttons on her cardigan as she hurried down the corridor towards the lift. Suddenly, without warning, the door opposite Mrs Stuckey's apartment opened and out stepped a young man. Hollie collied into him.

"I'm so sorry, I wasn't looking," she began.

"No, sorry, it was my fault. I stepped out into the corridor without looking." He paused while his eyes connected with hers then took a step back. "Please, after you."

He smiled, waiting for her to walk past. Hollie noticed his soft smile and brown eyes which had caught her attention, although she didn't want them to. She continued to look at him. He seemed to be in his early twenties, wore smart clothes, his curly hair just resting on his shoulders.

Hollie felt embarrassed that she had paused for so long and quickly walked past him. He closed his front door and walked up the corridor behind her. She decided to take the stairs to avoid the awkwardness of being in the lift with him. She looked at her watch as she hurried down the stairs. Footsteps behind her alerted her that he, too, was taking the stairs.

"I'm Samson. You must be my neighbour." He had caught her up.

Hollie turned round to him. It was never in her nature not to be polite to anyone.

"Hi, I'm Hollie. Have you just moved in? That place has been sitting empty for months."

"Yeah, yesterday. My parents bought it. They buy properties around the city to rent out. I usually stay in them while I renovate them before we find new tenants."

Hollie continued to hurry down the stairs.

"Does the apartment need a lot of work?"

"Not much – some painting, a new bathroom and a new kitchen. Shouldn't take long, maybe a couple of months."

Hollie caught hold of the handrail as she turned the corner, continuing down the last few stairs. He seemed like he had a happy-go-lucky life, paid for by Mum and Dad, she thought. I expect there's a model girlfriend moving in with him to match his lifestyle.

"I live next door with my boyfriend, Marcus. Mrs Stuckey lives across the hallway to you. She lost her husband a couple of months ago."

"Ah yes, I knocked on her door yesterday. Lovely lady – she invited me in for a cup of tea."

Hollie looked surprised and turned round briefly. Not many people could be bothered to check on dear old Mrs Stuckey. She was the only one in the whole block who regularly checked on her. They reached the bottom of the stairs.

"That was nice of you."

Samson opened the front door, holding it open for Hollie.

"She's given me a shopping list." He pulled out a piece of paper and handed it to Hollie. She smiled as she read through the list. Mrs Stuckey had written several female items that Hollie knew he would struggle with. They stepped out onto the pavement.

"Do you even know what lavender oil is?" Hollie handed him back the list

Samson put the list back in his pocket.

"Can't be that difficult. I'll just ask the shop assistant." They stood facing each other on the pavement.

"Good luck with the shopping – I must rush off, I'm late for work."

Samson smiled.

"Bye Hollie. Maybe I'll see you."

She smiled back. He was quite a handsome fellow.

"Maybe."

Hollie began to walk along Albert Street, crossing the road at the end, walking quickly. Thank goodness, she thought, that Marcus hadn't left the apartment at the same time as her that morning. He wouldn't have liked Samson talking to her. Maybe she would get to meet Samson's girlfriend soon. It would be nice to have a girl her own age living next door. Hollie turned the corner and walked in through the door of BB's Diner. She had never really known what BB's stood for, other than one of the Bs surely stood for Bob. Hollie had always assumed that the other B had been his wife's initial, who had left him some years ago. As she went through the restaurant, some other waitresses were preparing the tables for the lunchtime rush. She walked past the juke box and under the archway at the back and down the stairs into the cellar where she hung up her bag and cardigan.

The familiar smells of freshly ground coffee and cooked breakfast greeted her as she walked back through the restaurant, still tying the strings of her apron behind her. Hollie often worked behind the bar, making all the coffees, teas and cold drinks on a busy lunchtime. She went to find Bob.

"Morning, Bob, is everything alright?"

Bob was reaching retirement age. He had owned BB's Diner for over twenty years, the last few years on his own. It was all he had; he had no children, no close family. He opened the restaurant six days a week and worked six days a week. He was the first to get to work and the last to leave. Hollie thought it was sad he had no one to share it with, but he never grumbled; he was always happy.

"Hello Hollie, how lovely to see you. Your look particularly happy this morning. Did you have a good night with Beth?"

"I did, thanks Bob, we had a lovely meal. It was so nice to catch up with her. I haven't seen much of her since our university term finished."

"I'm glad. You deserved a good night out. You've worked so hard recently." Bob passed her some containers of sliced lemons and oranges. "Can you work the bar over lunchtime? I think we will be busy today."

"Of course." Hollie took the containers from him

18

and began to get stocked up, making several trips down to the cellar to bring enough supplies up to stock up the drinks bar. Some of the other waitresses rushed about, setting up the tables ready for lunch. The bar was next to the kitchen but, unlike the kitchen where the waitresses collected the meals from a hot plate, the bar had a separate hatchway that looked out into the diner. Hollie liked this, as she could see out, giving her a good indication when it was getting busy or beginning to go quiet.

Lunchtime started slowly, but soon larger tables came in, the waitresses rushing from table to table taking orders and carrying drinks and food. The menu was varied: snacks, salads, burgers and steaks. Lunchtime was always busy, with customers wanting to get served quickly during their lunch break. Hollie was very efficient preparing drinks and sometimes, if she had caught up with the bar orders and the other waitresses were busy, she would help by taking drinks to the tables.

Towards the end of lunchtime, Hollie took out a large drinks order on a tray to a table who were having a second round of drinks. When she got there, she called out each drink, waiting for the customer to claim it then reaching over to place it in front of them. The table was made up of young people, all laughing and chatting, so she found herself raising her voice to make herself heard. She looked for a space to place the last drink on the table, then looked up as she heard a thank you. She was looking at Samson.

"Hello again, I didn't think I would see you so soon." Samson took the glass from her.

Hollie stood still for a moment, wishing now that she had stayed behind the bar.

"Hello, again." The two girls either side of him didn't look pleased that he had spoken to her. They were staring at her, wanting her to go away. One of the girls pushed their empty glass towards Hollie.

"I'll have another white wine spritzer, waitress."

Samson turned to the girl next to him.

"This isn't the waitress who takes the orders – you need to wait for the other girl."

"It's alright, I can get you another drink." Hollie took the empty glass, placing it on her tray, then returned to the bar. What a coincidence that Samson had come to the diner for lunch. She felt strangely awkward when he looked at her. She was sure that one of the girls sat next to him was his girlfriend.

Hollie returned to the table with the girl's drink, deciding not to look at Samson this time. He was laughing with his friend across the table when she approached. She placed the glass in front of the girl, who didn't acknowledge Hollie.

Samson looked up.

"Thank you, Hollie," he said, looking embarrassed at his girl's rudeness.

Another of Samson's friends across the table looked at Hollie.

"We should come here more often for the fabulous food and hot stuff to serve us."

Before Hollie had chance to react, Samson learned over the table.

"Shut up, Seb, don't talk to her like that." Immediately Seb's face changed; he didn't like being spoken to like that by Samson.

"Sorry," he said to Hollie. "I didn't mean anything by it."

"It's OK, really," she said and smiled at him. She could feel the eyes of the two girls sitting either side of Samson staring at her with fury now and was hoping that neither one was his girlfriend. She knew that Samson was looking at her as she walked away but she didn't want to embarrass herself further by making eye contact once again. As soon as she returned to the bar, she breathed a sigh of relief and hoped that Bob didn't swap her with one of the other waitresses so that she would have to work the floor and possibly see Samson again. Thankfully, and much to Hollie's relief, she remained on the bar until the end of her shift. Bob plated her up a roast dinner and wrapped it in foil.

"Thank you for today, Hollie. No matter how busy we are, you never get flustered and always get through those orders. What would I do without you?" Hollie kissed him on the cheek. Bob was such a kind, sweet old man

"Thanks, Bob. I'll see you tomorrow."

Hollie walked slowly home. She knew Marcus wouldn't be home till after 5 o'clock, so she had enough time to pop in to Mrs Stuckey's, give her the roast dinner and sort out her washing.

She took the lift to the third floor. Her feet were tired today. She knocked as usual and went straight into Mrs Stuckey's apartment.

"Hello, Mrs Stuckey?" she called out, walking down the hall and straight ahead into the kitchen. She was expecting to see the old lady sitting as usual at the kitchen table reading or looking at photos. There were shopping bags half unpacked on the kitchen table. Samson must have got her shopping that she had asked for. Hollie was tempted to have a quick look in the bags, curious to know if he had got everything on her list. Surely he couldn't have possibly got everything correct? Hollie took a step closer to the bags to peer inside when she heard Mrs Stuckey's voice call out.

"Is that you, Hollie?" She sounded distressed. Hollie quickly went to find her.

"Where are you, Mrs Stuckey?"

"I'm in the bedroom, my dear," she replied, her voice trembling.

Hollie immediately rushed in, to find the elderly lady laying between her dressing table and her bed.

"Oh Mrs Stuckey, whatever has happened?" Hollie leant over to get closer to her. "Can you get up if I help you?"

"I think I tripped over the end of the eiderdown that was hanging too far down. I'll try but I think I'm quite wedged down here."

Hollie tried to lift her, but it was no good. Mrs Stuckey didn't have room to move her legs to get herself to her knees.

"I need to go and get some help. Don't worry, I'll come straight back."

Hollie got up and hurried out of the front door and into the hall, leaving Mrs Stuckey lying on the floor. First, she went to her own apartment to see if Marcus had got home early. She unlocked the front door.

"Marcus, are you home?" she called out. There was no sign of his work shoes. She knew they would be lined up neatly with his other shoes.

She went back into the hallway, thinking about who else would be home this time of the day. Most of the tenants in the block were working couples. She reached Mrs Stuckey's door, then turning to look at Samson's door. Hollie reluctantly knocked; she knew he must be home as he had dropped off Mrs Stuckey's shopping.

A moment later, the door opened to reveal Samson, wearing only a pair of dark grey joggers, no socks, no top. Hollie had never seen such broad shoulders, with muscles bulging from his neck down. He smiled at her.

"Hi."

There was a moment of silence. Hollie tried to imagine that he was dressed as he was earlier when she saw him, trying not to look at any part of him below his chin.

"I need your help. Mrs Stuckey has fallen and I can't get her up."

His smile changed to concern.

"I'll just grab a top." He went back into his apartment, then came out pulling a T-shirt over his head – this was less of a distraction for Hollie. She was relieved he had been home. He followed Hollie back into Mrs Stuckey's apartment and into her bedroom.

"Mrs Stuckey," Hollie called out to her. "Samson is with me; he's going to help me lift you up."

Samson leaned over the old lady, placing both his

arms underneath her, then lifted her with ease, like a precious child. He placed her carefully, sitting her up on the bed.

"Thank you both. I feel so silly. I just came into the bedroom to put some things away when I tripped. What an old fool I am."

"Don't be silly, Mrs Stuckey. Let us help you back into the kitchen. I'll put your shopping away and make you a cup of tea. Are you sure you're not hurt?"

Samson put out his arm for Mrs Stuckey to take hold of.

"I think I'm alright, my dear," she said, shuffling forward and taking hold of Samson's arm. Hollie watched as he carefully and patiently walked her slowly into the kitchen. He helped her into the chair beside the kitchen table, then sat down beside her.

"This lovely young man lives across the hallway, Hollie. Have you met him before?"

Hollie looked at Samson.

"Yes, I bumped into him in the hall this morning." She turned away, filling the kettle with water, then switched it on.

"Two sugars for me, Hollie," Samson said. Hollie turned around quickly. He had done what she had asked; now it was his cue to leave, so she and Mrs Stuckey could have a chat. She looked at him. But he had no intention of going just yet – he was staying for his cup of tea. Hollie began to put the shopping away while she waited for the kettle to boil. She stirred the two sugars into his tea then placed it in front of him.

"Thank you." He looked at her with a soft smile. She looked back at him not wanting to return the gesture. The moment was interrupted by the old lady.

"He is a good shopper, isn't he Hollie?" Mrs Stuckey said looking at Samson. "We are fortunate that you have moved in on to our floor, aren't we?"

Hollie took a sip of her tea.

"Yes, very fortunate." Hollie looked at Samson. She wasn't too sure that they needed a macho fellow who probably already had a big ego.

"I'll only be here for about eight weeks. I have to fit a new bathroom and kitchen, then redecorate the whole apartment before the apartment is let. Then I'll move on." He looked at Mrs Stuckey. "Please, while I'm here, let me know if you need any odd jobs doing"

Hollie put the washing into the tumble dryer. It might be nice to have someone else to help her with looking after Mrs Stuckey, even if only for a few weeks.

Hollie knew that Mrs Stuckey would certainly enjoy having the extra company. She was thrilled when Hollie and Marcus had moved in at the end of the hallway. Hollie made friends with Mr and Mrs Stuckey that very first day. Marcus wanted to unpack his things and put everything in the flat where he thought it would be best, but Hollie didn't care for unpacking; instead, she knocked on the Stuckey's door just to introduce herself and say hello. She stayed all afternoon. Hollie had been awfully close to Mrs Stuckey ever since. She was unsure of Samson's intentions. He too must have called in on Mrs Stuckey this morning to introduce himself – why else would he end up with a shopping list? Now he was sitting chatting with her as though he had known her for years. Mrs Stuckey did seem to like him very much, though. Hollie was unsure of most men; they had the ability to manipulate any situation to gain the authority and take control, which was so often the case.

Samson stood up.

"I must get back now. You know where to find me if you need anything." He wrote his phone number on a piece of paper in the kitchen then looked at Hollie. She stopped drying the dishes.

"Thank you, Samson," she said, finally giving him the smile that he wanted.

"Anytime, Hollie. Maybe I'll see you again." He walked towards the door. Hollie hoped that she wouldn't see him again. If Marcus saw him smiling at her and her smiling back, there would be hell to pay.

Certainly not worth the risk.

When Samson had gone, Hollie washed up the last few things.

"Are you sure you're going to be alright?"

"Yes, my dear, you get home to that boyfriend of yours, he'll be wondering where you are."

Hollie picked up her bag and cardigan.

"I'll call on you the day after tomorrow. I'm working late tomorrow at the diner. Call me, though, if you want anything." Hollie leaned over to give the old lady a kiss on the cheek.

"Bye, my dear Hollie."

Hollie closed Mrs Stuckey's door and walked down the hallway to her own front door. She looked at her watch – it was twenty past five. Marcus would certainly be home now. His accountancy firm was only a ten minute walk from the apartment, one of the reasons he had chosen this flat for them. Hollie opened the front door. Glancing down, she could see Marcus's shoes lined up in pairs, his shiny black work shoes at the end. Hollie took off hers and placed them neatly on her row, next to her favourite pumps.

"Hello?" she called out. Hollie walked into the front room. Marcus wasn't there, but the table was neatly laid for tea with a bottle of wine. The front room overlooked Albert Street. She went over to the window; it was a gorgeous warm summer evening. The street was still busy with people hurrying to go home, buses and cars weaving their way up and down the street.

"There you are." She turned away from the window when she heard his voice and smiled at him. He walked across the room towards her, putting his hand on her cheek, then kissed her.

"I'm sorry for being angry with you last night." Hollie didn't reply. "I just get so worried about you and then get so cross when you come home drunk. You're such a beautiful girl that I worry about other men showing interest in you when I'm not there to look after you."

Marcus went over to the table, opened the bottle of wine from the table, then poured them both a glass. Hollie knew that she hadn't been drunk the night before but was guilty only of enjoying an evening of laughter with her best friend, something that she had missed out on recently.

"Please, come and sit down. I've made you your favourite tea: moussaka and garlic bread." Marcus pulled out the chair, so Hollie sat down.

"This looks lovely and the moussaka smells great." She took a sip of her wine; moussaka wasn't really her favourite. Soon after they had first met, Marcus took her to an Italian restaurant. When they arrived, late in the evening, the restaurant had been very busy. The waiter gave them the menu, then listed all the menu choices that they had run out of. Moussaka was one of the dishes that they had lots of. Hollie could see Marcus was getting annoyed with the waiter and was about to raise his voice, so to calm the situation Hollie had told the waiter she was delighted that they hadn't run out of moussaka as it was her favourite dish. Ever since then, Marcus thought moussaka was her favourite meal which made her smile. Being a Cornish girl from a small fishing village, she would have to put the pasty above all other food, but only her mum back down south would know that.

Marcus placed their plates in front of them, waiting for Hollie's approval in return for his efforts. Hollie began to eat, not wanting to discuss the night before. Knowing that Marcus now thought he had made amends, she decided to talk about something else.

"How was your day?"

"My day went fantastically well, thank you," Marcus began. "My breakfast meeting with some potential clients was a success. The boss was very impressed with how I handled it – in fact, so impressed that he then took me out to lunch to congratulate me."

Hollie was pleased that he was making such a good impression at his firm. He had worked hard for this promotion. Marcus continued to talk about the rest of his day, telling Hollie every detail, not once, though, asking about how her day at the diner had been. He only stopped briefly to return to the kitchen to get their dessert – lime cheesecake, Marcus's favourite. After they had both done the washing-up, which Marcus always insisted they did before they relax in the front room, they sat on the sofa for the remainder of the evening.

Just before ten, Hollie got up and kissed Marcus on the head.

"Goodnight, I'm off to bed. Don't forget I'm on a split shift tomorrow so I won't finish till ten."

Marcus looked up at her.

"I'll be glad when you finish that job after the summer. You can't go into the final year of your degree still working in that bloody diner. You need to concentrate on your studies."

Hollie heard his voice starting to get louder. She really didn't want to give up working at the diner.

"Let's discuss it tomorrow."

"I'll pick you up at ten sharp. Make sure you come straight out. I'll be waiting outside."

Hollie smiled to acknowledge him, turning to go into the bedroom. She hoped that Marcus would finish watching the film and not follow her. She was tired and wanted to go to sleep. Fortunately, he didn't.

Chapter Three

Hollie rushed out of the apartment like any typical morning, still sipping her coffee in her plastic cup. She never got up early enough to allow herself enough time to enjoy breakfast and coffee at home before leaving for work. She pushed the heel of her pumps on as she locked the front door, hurried up the hallway, passing Mrs Stuckey's apartment, then Samson's opposite, walking quickly and quietly, not wanting to bump into him again. Three encounters yesterday were more than enough. She was relieved to make it to the lift. Her journey to work was a quick brisk walk, usually taking her just over ten minutes. Bob opened at 10 o'clock; usually, she walked in just as the news was coming on the radio in the staffroom in the cellar. Bob never minded, though. He would be in the kitchen prepping and didn't always notice her punctuality. Hollie always made him a mug of coffee in the morning and took it to him in the kitchen where he had been working for several hours. The diner was laid out with most of its tables in rows and high backs to each bench seat. The colours were all bright and the décor was mainly blue, red and green. Many students came in at lunchtimes as the main campus was only a fifteen minute walk away. During the summer months, though, lots of tourists came in for lunch and snacks which Hollie preferred they tipped more generously.

She went in and when some of the other waitresses had arrived for work, she went into the kitchen to see if Bob needed any help. A couple of kitchen assistants would be arriving for work shortly.

"The girls are filling the sugars up and writing the blackboard. Everything else is ready for lunch. Do you want me to come in here to help?"

"Thank you, Hollie. Could you start chopping that salad over by the sink? The boys will be here in a bit."

Hollie washed her hands then went over to start chopping the salad.

"You look a little sad today, Hollie. Is everything alright at home?"

Bob certainly knew Hollie well. He had seen her through good days and bad days, never asking for any details that she wasn't prepared to give.

"I'm fine, Bob, really."

Hollie didn't like to burden him with her problems. He couldn't fix them anyway. He had his own worries – he was trying to run a business on his own, no wife, no family. No-one to share the stress of life with, nor the success that BB's had become.

The lunch rush started early. Hollie took charge of the restaurant – this involved waiting on tables but also being the first to greet customers at the front door. She usually had the time to show them to a free table or, at the very least, point them in the direction of an unoccupied table. She had a pleasant, well-mannered nature and always worked with a smile on her face. No matter what the situation, she could always deal with it – even the rudest customers. Her natural kindness reduced people's anger about whatever was wrong and her infectious smile encouraged others to smile too. Bob had spotted this about her on her first day. He would be sad if ever she decided to leave. She never had a lunch break till after Bob – he always left her in charge while he took his break. She was popular with the other waitresses, so they didn't mind her taking charge and giving them orders instead of Bob.

Bob had employed two kitchen assistants from Sir Lanka, Sashimi and Rashmi, brothers in their late teens. Sadly, the brothers had recently lost both parents and had come to England to live with their uncle. He already had five children and grandparents, all cramped into a small two bed terrace house. The brothers were of working age, and so their uncle wanted them to get jobs to help bring some money into the household. It wasn't long after Bob's wife had left him, and he wasn't coping emotionally or physically. When the boys came into the restaurant with their uncle, Bob said he would give them both a job working in the kitchen. Sashimi and Rashmi didn't disappoint. They quickly learnt to cook everything on the menu and worked as many hours as possible. After the first year, the tenants above the restaurant gave notice and moved out. Bob let Sashimi and Rashmi move into the now vacant flat at a reduced rent. The brothers were so grateful for a place of their own, a bedroom of their own.

Both boys adored Hollie – she was so patient with them, always helping them with their English, especially when they didn't understand important letters and legal documents, like applying for UK citizenship.

The busy lunchtime rush began to quieten off. After Bob had been for a break, Hollie took hers. She walked across the road to the park opposite the diner, placed her cardigan on the grass then sat on it to eat the sandwich that Bob had prepared for her. The sun was shining, and the park was busy with families and couples having picnics, playing games or, just like Hollie, enjoying a peaceful moment in the sunshine.

|She lay back, resting her head on the soft grass. Looking up at the blue sky while the sun warmed her skin, she could have been anywhere. Her thoughts were of that evening, talking to Marcus. She knew that she had to tell him that she wasn't prepared to give up her waitress job at the diner. Why did she have to convince him anyway? She knew that her degree wouldn't suffer because of her working part time – it hadn't these past three years, and anyway, it wasn't his decision to make. Hollie was determined to make him understand how important this job was too her. Surly if Marcus genuinely loved her, he would let her make her own choice?

She returned to the restaurant where the evening shift started slowly. It wasn't long though before people began to come in and soon the diner was full which Hollie loved because the shift always went so quickly. Bob hadn't expected it to be quite as busy, so hadn't arranged enough waiting staff. Hollie kept everything running smoothly front of house. She knew the kitchen staff would be working very quickly to keep churning out the meals at a constant rate. She kept her eye on the clock as last orders were at 9 o'clock. This evening, a couple of tables had come in close to nine and had been in no rush to order or eat and then wanted dessert. It was gone ten before she took their payment on the till. That was her last job, to make sure everyone had paid up; then she could finish.

Conscious of the time, Hollie rushed down to the cellar to get her bag and cardigan, removing her apron and stuffing it into her bag on the way back up the stairs. She felt tired; it had been a long day.

"Good night, Bob, see you in a couple of days." She had two days off now and was looking forward to them.

Bob put his head out though the kitchen door. "Thank you, Hollie, see you then."

She looked at her watch; Marcus had been waiting for fifteen minutes and she knew he wouldn't be pleased. Maybe tonight wouldn't be a good time to talk about her keeping her job at the diner. She spotted him on the other side of the road, leaning against the wall, both hands in his pockets.

She hurried over to him. "I'm so sorry, Marcus, the last few customers took so long to finish up and pay." She could see as she got closer to him, even though the street was dark, that he was cross.

"Come on, let's go home," he said and started to walk quickly. Hollie, not wanting to anger him further, said nothing and walked quickly beside him. Maybe, she thought, he would be calmer once they got home. As they turned the corner into Albert Street, it began to rain. Up ahead, she could see a group of people on the pavement, gathered outside their apartment block. When they got closer, she could hear them saying goodbye, then one of them walked up the steps and into their building. Hollie and Marcus followed closely behind them. Suddenly Hollie realised it was Samson in front of them and he was now waiting for the lift to come down.

Hollie quickly took hold of Marcus's hand. "Let's take the stairs, the lift will be ages."

Marcus looked at her while walking towards the lift. "You're joking. I've been working all day, stood waiting for you for bloody ages. Do you really think I want to walk up three flights of stairs?"

The lift door opened. Samson stepped in turning to press floor three, then seeing Marcus and Hollie he pressed the button to hold the door open and waited while they walked in. Samson looked at Marcus. "What floor, mate?"

Hollie could hear her heart beating quickly and loudly, racing with fear that Samson would start chatting to her about yesterday. Bumping into him in the morning, seeing her at the diner at lunchtime, then having a cup of tea with him at Mrs Stuckey's, all of which she had said nothing to Marcus about. Hollie waited for her nightmare to begin. She had no idea how she would explain this. Marcus would think she had been lying to him.

"Floor three please, mate," Marcus said, glancing briefly to Samson.

Samson pressed for floor three, then kept his eyes looking forward at the lift door in silence.

When the doors opened, he held out his hand. "After you."

Marcus walked out first. "Cheers, mate."

Hollie breathed a sigh of relief as she stepped out of the lift. Glancing back to Samson, she smiled at him. He looked at her for the first time that evening, his eyes fixed on only her. His soft smile appeared. No words were exchanged between them. Hollie turned away and caught up with Marcus down the hallway before he noticed that she wasn't behind him.

He appeared to have calmed down when they got into the apartment. He placed his shoes neatly in their place, next to his work shoes that were always at the end of the row. He had an early start the next morning, so she was expecting him to go to bed. Instead, he went into the kitchen and poured himself a large glass of red wine. Hollie went into the front room where she switched on the television. She was tired and wanted to go to bed but thought she would sit with Marcus for a short while. He followed her, sitting down on the settee beside her.

"I wish you wouldn't work so late. It's always such a fuss to come and get you, especially when I've been working all day."

"Marcus, I've told you, it's kind of you to come

and meet me, but really I can walk back by myself. It's only ten minutes along roads that are lit with streetlamps." Hollie knew where this conversation was leading. She was determined not to be bullied into leaving – she enjoyed working at BB's Diner, she enjoyed meeting new people, she loved working for Bob, they had become such good friends over these past few years. She was sad to think that she wouldn't be able to continue helping Sashimi and Rashmi with their English. Hollie didn't want to leave just because Marcus wanted her to.

"Marcus," she continued, having suddenly found some confidence. "I won't quit. I enjoy working at the diner. If it will make you feel better, I'll ask Bob if I could have fewer late shifts."

Marcus stood up. "Make me feel better?" His voice became louder. "It would make me feel bloody better if you were to leave that diner!"

Hollie's confidence suddenly disappeared as his face locked in anger.

"I've told you – I don't want you working there anymore. People telling you what to do all day, men staring at you while you serve them."

"Don't be silly, Marcus, men don't stare at me."

"I've seen them. You're too flirty and friendly with them. Then they get the wrong idea about you."

"What are you talking about, Marcus?" Hollie stood up. "I've heard enough – I'm off to bed."

She turned to walk out of the room. Marcus was now full of fury, but she wasn't submissive to him. This wasn't the usual way she delt with Marcus's raging outbursts; normally, she would have backed down way before now.

"You'll tell Bob that this is your last week."

Hollie knew her head was telling her that now she should surrender and back down before his anger exploded into something that neither of them wanted to test. The next few words just flowed out from her mouth. Her usually sensible head hadn't taken control.

"No, I will not."

Marcus couldn't accept these words. His face became wild with anger and he threw his wine glass towards her. It smashed against the wall beside her. Fear immediately raced through her and she knew she had to get out of the apartment. She ran across the front room to the door. Marcus got there first, grabbing her arm, pulling her back. Thrashing at him, she fought to get away, but she was no match for Marcus. She tried to pull the door open with all the strength she had but it was no use as he held the door shut with one hand. With no warning, his other hand came towards her, hitting the side of her face, knocking her across the room. She hit the wall hard then dropped to the floor. Her face landed where the broken glass had fallen. She froze, lying still, as she could feel her face becoming wet and knew that she was bleeding. Her heart was beating quicker than it ever had before and she was filled with anger and fear. Her head now took control at last and she knew she must lie still, knowing that Marcus would calm down and back away from hurting her again. She couldn't understand – how had it come to this? She must have seen the signs and knew this was coming, but could she have stopped it? Why had she not left him a long time ago? Many thoughts were rushing round her head but for now she knew she must lie still and say nothing; she knew she couldn't fight him off. Marcus stood still for a moment then stepped closer to her.

"Why do you make me so mad that I lose my temper with you? Do you do it on purpose, to see how far you can push me?"

A loud knock came from the front door.

"Who the hell can that be?" Marcus, still fuelled with rage, left Hollie lying pitifully on the floor. He hurried to the front door.

"Hey, mate, I'm Samson from across the hallway. I heard a lot of shouting and banging – I just wanted to check you guys were alright."

Marcus clearly didn't want him interfering and just

wanted to get rid of him. "Yeah, we're fine, thanks," he said as he began to close the door. Samson placed his foot into the frame, stopping the door from closing.

"I'll go when I've seen that Hollie's alright." Samson pushed the door open with his hand.

Marcus was furious. "GET OUT!" he shouted.

Samson knew something was wrong and stepped further into the apartment. Marcus took a step closer to him, swinging his fist toward him. Samson caught it like a tennis ball in one hand, his other hand clenching into a fist which he swung towards Marcus, knocking him across the room. Samson walked into the front room where he saw Hollie lying on the floor. He picked her up carefully in his arms, her bloody face pressed against his chest, and walked towards the front door. Marcus still lay on the floor, holding his nose which was now bleeding.

Samson walked past him. "You don't deserve her."

He walked out of the front door with Hollie in his arms, straight passed his apartment door and down the stairs. Hollie was silent; she still couldn't believe what had just happened. Her body was shaking with fear. He held her close to him as he felt her body tremble.

"Please don't be scared anymore. You're safe now. I don't want to take you back to my apartment, it's too close to him. There's an empty apartment across town that my parents own. They've just let it out to a couple on a six-month lease. Unfortunately, they have had to return to Dubai on business so had to leave at short notice. The apartment is empty. You can stay there a while."

Hollie remained silent. Marcus was once a kind man who would do nice things for her. She had loved him and thought that he had loved her too. She felt so foolish.

Samson's truck, a white double cab Mitsubishi, was parked just a minute's walk up the street. He opened the door and placed her carefully in the front seat, fastening the seatbelt securely around her. He reached into the back seat for an old jacket, tucking it around her. Blood was still dripping from her lip, running down her chin. He got in quickly and started the engine. During the ten-minute drive, Hollie remained silent. Samson looked at her every chance he could take his eyes off the road. He was unsure if she needed medical attention but decided to get her somewhere she could feel safe and then ring for a doctor to come and check her. After a short drive across town, he stopped alongside the pavement next to some tall railings that seemed to be the perimeter of a park. It was dark with not much street lighting. He came round and picked her up in his arms once more, holding her close to his chest, as he walked a short distance along the street, then up a few steps to a front door. He tapped the code into the keypad to gain access then carried her up three floors. When they got to the top, he used a swipe card to open the apartment door. Hollie had her head tucked close to his chest so didn't see much more than a grand hallway with beautiful pictures and décor. Samson took her into a double bedroom, just off the hallway. He lay her on the bed, trying to prop her up a little with the ridiculous number of pillows and cushions that decorated the bed then he disappeared for a couple of minutes. When he returned, he had some towels, warm water and some cotton strips. With tender gentleness, he dipped the cotton strips into the warm water. Slowly and carefully, he cleaned the blood from her face. It became obvious that the blood was coming from a large cut on her lip, caused by the broken glass, and her eye had now started to swell up. Samson carefully held a cold ice-pack above it. Still Hollie was silent and motionless. Samson reached in his pocket for his phone and got straight through to the doctor.

He turned to face her, his T-shirt covered in blood.

"I'm just going to pop down to the truck. I've got some old clothes in the back. I think I must have something that will fit you. I'll be straight back."

Hollie heard the front door close; she lay still, just lifting her head up a little. The bedroom was large and a beautiful white dressing table caught her eye. She

45

had never seen such a fabulous piece of furniture with its detail of flower petals around the edge of the mirror which then became entwined ivy down each leg, all made from wood. The furthest wall had small silver handles running from one side to the other. She was intrigued to know what cupboards and wardrobes were hidden behind. The door of the ensuite was open, enough for Hollie to see a pure white corner bath sitting on a luxurious marble floor. Across the hallway, she could make out another bedroom.

She heard the front door open, then Samson appeared, taking off his blood-stained T-shirt and throwing it on the floor. He put on another T-shirt and sat down on the bed beside her, passing her a hoodie. She was still wearing her waitress's uniform but blood had soaked into the material. She sat up, taking the hoodie.

"Thanks," she said, then shuffled back on the bed, beginning to unzip her dress at the back. She stopped and looked at Samson who then realised she was waiting for him to leave while she got out of her blood-stained clothes.

"Sorry," he said, feeling awkward. "I'll go and get you a glass of water while you're getting changed." He left the room for a few minutes, returning with a glass of water. She was wearing his hoodie, her hair no longer tied up but hanging down to her shoulders. He pulled the duvet cover up to cover her to her waist then sat back beside her.

"Do you want me to leave you alone for a while?"

Hollie shook her head.

"Shall I ring your mum or one of your friends to come sit with you?"

The thought of her mother knowing what had happened was horrifying for Hollie. She would be so upset and worried, especially as they were so far away.

"Thank you, but not just yet," she said. She had only known him for two days and here she was in his apartment, on his bed, wearing his clothes, looking like a mess.

"I'm so sorry," she began. "You shouldn't have…"

"Please don't say sorry." He moved his hand to touch hers, then pulled back, resting his hand on the bed near hers. He didn't want to touch her.

"I feel such a fool. Deep down, I knew he had anger issues and would lose his temper, but I never thought that it would be with me." She swept her hair from her face. Samson could see her eye had swollen a little more; her lip had stopped bleeding but had now become swollen too.

"Everyone sees him as a kind, macho, well-mannered guy, but really he's just a controlling asshole. We were arguing because he wanted me to quit my job – he said it was because he wanted me to concentrate on my degree but really it was because he didn't want me mixing with my friends from the diner. He wanted control over who I saw and what I did. I'm so stupid." Tears filled her eyes. Samson couldn't bear to see her cry and took hold of her hand as gently as he could, then with his other hand he wiped her tears away.

The doorbell buzzed. "That must be the doctor." He got up and she could hear them talking in the hallway, following which a mature man with a doctor's bag came into the room. Samson stood just in the doorway to the bedroom, not wanting to leave Hollie alone with anyone she didn't know.

The doctor checked her over, paying particular attention to the gash on her lip. He closed his bag then began to write out a prescription.

"That is a nasty gash – I'm writing you out a prescription for some ointment to help keep that clean and some penicillin. It will take a few days for the swelling on your lip and that bump over your eye to go down. Ring me back if anything changes," he said, handing Samson the prescription. Samson thanked him for coming out so quickly and walked with him to the front door.

Minutes later, he returned to Hollie.

"Can I get you anything?"

Hollie smiled at him. "No thank you. I feel so

tired, I think I'll try to get some sleep." She put her head on the pillow, feeling exhausted; it was gone midnight.

Samson pulled the duvet up to cover her, then picked up the blood-stained clothes from the floor. He leant down beside her, switching off the bedside lamp.

"I'll be across the hallway if you need me."

Hollie looked at him and smiled, then closed her eyes.

Chapter Four

Hollie woke the next morning to her lip throbbing. It was a sudden reminder off the events from the night before. She turned her head slightly to see Samson asleep on the floor beside her. He lay on a mattress that he must have dragged in from the other bedroom from across the hallway. Wearing only the trousers that he had been wearing the previous night, she could see he was sleeping peacefully, his head resting on his pillow. As he was lying on his front, she could see his back and upper arms had several tattoos. She didn't want to wake him but she wanted to get up. Remembering she was wearing only Samson's hoodie, she stood up quietly to see how long it was. She smiled in relief when she noticed it came halfway down her thighs.

She walked quietly over to the shutters, opening them just enough to look outside but not to let too much light in to wake Samson. For a moment, she was taken aback by such a fabulous view of the city. When Samson had driven her here last night, she had no sense of where he was driving, but now, looking out across the city, she could see they were on Nelson's Hill, an awfully expensive part of town. In front of the window was a Juliet balcony. She could only imagine the view on a summer morning. Just across the road, she could see a beautiful park with wooden benches dotted along the path, where a man was walking his dog; she watched him walk into the distance as he went over a little bridge that crossed a stream. The sun was already shining high in the sky, so she knew she had woken late. Hollie stood for a few minutes longer, enjoying the quiet moment and beautiful view. She left the shutters a little open and tiptoed quietly past Samson to the bathroom.

She closed the door then paused before looking in the mirror. Her lip had now swollen and the lump over her eye was a deep blue, nearly black. She took a deep breath, not knowing what to do next. She knew she must ring Beth this morning. Maybe she could go stay with her for a while. Beth's parents adored Hollie, so that was a good option. The start of her final year at university started in a few weeks so she would need to find somewhere close by to rent. There was always student accommodation on the university campus. But she couldn't do much today – there was no way she wanted to face the world with her face looking like this. She went back to sit on the bed for a while, pulling the covers over her legs.

Samson turned over, opening his eyes and looking up towards Hollie nestled amongst the cushions and pillows. He looked at her pretty face, her long hair draped over her shoulders, wearing just his hoodie.

"Did you sleep well?" he asked as he sat up. "I pulled the mattress in so I could be here if you woke in the night and needed anything."

Hollie smiled. "I slept well, thank you."

Hollie tried not to look at his upper body, now in full view in front of her.

"Do you need me to ring the diner or anyone – are you due in to work today?" He reached for his T-shirt, pulling it over his head, then stood up.

"No, I'm off for two days. I'll see how my face looks after that before I decide if I should go back on Thursday."

Samson dragged his mattress back into the other bedroom and returned with her waitress pinafore neatly folded, her mobile phone and purse resting on top. He placed them on the bed beside her. Hollie smiled.

"I washed them out last night. Your phone and purse were in the pocket of your dress."

· Hollie stared at the items for a moment. These

were the only items that she now possessed. Everything else was back in the apartment with Marcus. She knew that she would probably never see any of her belongings again.

"Do you want me to go back and get the rest of your things?"

"No, definitely not. I can buy new stuff, new clothes. I never want to see him again." Hollie picked up her phone.

"I might ring Beth – my best friend – in a bit. She'll bring me over some clothes. Just till I can get to the shops and buy some new ones. What girl wouldn't want to buy a whole new wardrobe?"

Samson could tell that she didn't really feel excited at the thought of that.

"I'll write down this address for you to give her." He looked around for a pen – not finding one, he headed for the kitchen.

"Would you like some coffee?"

Hollie threw the duvet off her legs. The thought of coffee certainly made her want to get up.

"I'd love some, thank you."

She followed him along the hallway and into an open plan lounge and dining area, with the kitchen leading off under an archway.

"Wow!" Hollie couldn't contain herself. She was in

a top floor corner penthouse apartment. Patio doors in front of her led out onto a roof terrace which appeared to have one of the best views across the city. The furniture was minimal and light in colour with a modern, elegant feel; everything was perfectly placed around the room. There were pure white shutters but they were so high up that no-one overlooked them. Hollie walked across the floor in her bare feet. The cold marble floor on her skin felt soothing as she headed, intrigued, towards the roof terrace.

"Go on. I'll bring your coffee out."

Hollie looked briefly at him.

"Alright," she said, trying not to show her excitement and eagerness to get out onto that terrace. She was in a truly gorgeous apartment. The heat from the sun hit her as she stepped out onto the terrace from where she could see for miles over the city. She sat down on one of the comfy outdoor chairs. For a moment, in the glorious sunshine, she forgot why she was there, the events of the night before, the injuries on her face, and just for a minute she enjoyed the moment.

Samson stepped out onto the terrace holding two mugs of coffee.

"Thank you," Hollie said and took the mug from him, smelling one of her favourite smells. "This place is quite spectacular. Do your parents really own it?"

Samson sat beside her. "Yeah, they own fifteen apartments across the city. This one is probably their most luxurious. It is mainly let on a short lease, usually to businesspeople who require a hotel-style apartment to fit their lifestyle – dining, business meetings, that sort of thing – while they're in the city on business."

"Your parents sound like they have done well with the property market to have such amazing apartments to rent out."

Samson put out his feet, resting them on an ornament plant pot.

"It's mainly my stepdad, Hector, who's built up their property empire. My mother left my dad when I was eight and my sister Sophia was six. We spent a year on our own, then my mother met Hector. He didn't have any children of his own and treated me like a son from the day I met him. Plus, he treated my mother like a princess every day till he married her and then she became his queen. He'd do anything for her."

Hollie tucked her legs beneath her. "He sounds such a lovely man"

"He's a great guy. He inherited some money when his uncle passed away and wisely invested it in a couple of properties that he renovated, then rented. He seemed to know what to look for each time he purchased another one, always buying something where he could see potential and make good."

Hollie carefully took a sip of her coffee, trying to not upset her lip. "And where do you fit in?"

"When I left college, I took an apprenticeship as an electrician with an electrical firm. When I was fully qualified, I began to help Hector at weekends with rewiring, putting in kitchens, bathrooms. Then I took plumbing at night school. Soon after, I gave up my job and worked with Hector fulltime. He's such a great bloke – he would do anything for my sister and me. How about your parents, are they close by?"

Hollie smiled at the thought of her parents. "My family are all in Cornwall. I don't get to see them much. Usually just a few days during holiday time, but I can never seem to stay for long."

"Do they visit you much?"

Hollie laughed. "My parents have never been over the Tamar Bridge. Mum has never wanted or needed to leave and Dad couldn't be dragged from his beloved Cornwall either. My two older sisters both still live at home. I left three years ago to come to London to do my veterinary degree. My family hope that I'll return to settle when I've graduated and take work as a vet back in Cornwall."

Samson smiled at her; she talked so fondly of her family. "You must miss them all. It must be hard to be so far away from them."

"I do, so very much, but I knew I had to leave to make a better life for myself. I have always wanted to become a vet and I couldn't achieve that by staying at home."

She took out her phone. "I better ring Beth now, to bring me over some clothes when she comes to pick me up."

Samson looked puzzled. "You know you can stay here; this place is empty. It hasn't even been advertised to be let again yet. Really, it will be empty for a while – you can stay here if you like. I'm going back to my apartment tonight, so the place is all yours."

"Samson, you've already done too much. Coming to get me last night, bringing me here. I can't expect you to do any more. I can stay with Beth till I go back to university. Then I'll get student accommodation on campus for my last year. It's close to BB's Diner so I'll still be able to work."

Samson picked up his empty mug from the ground. "You must decide to do whatever you feel is best." He stood up. "I've got to go back to the other apartment on Albert Street – there's an order of some kitchen tiles arriving there this morning but I should be back by mid-afternoon. Will you still be here?"

Hollie knew that he was only trying to help in

offering to let her stay here, but she thought it would be best if she stayed at Beth's for now. She didn't want to complicate things by staying in his apartment. "Yes, of course – I'll wait for you to get back before I go."

She followed him to the front door, where he showed her how to use the control pad to open the front door so she could let Beth into the building, and handed her a key card.

"This is the front door key, take it with you if you go out. You'll need it to get back in." He put on his work boots and picked up his keys from the small hallway sideboard. "Are you sure you'll be alright?"

"Yes, of course I'll be fine – go and do some work."

Samson smiled at her, then closed the door behind him.

Hollie learnt back on the door, gazing down the hallway. There was a beautiful vase sitting on a small shelf in an alcove in the wall. Paintings of modern art were dotted along the wall of the hallway, up to the archway that went into the lounge area. This place was more like a hotel than someone's home, she thought. She went into the lounge and sat on the corner sofa; it almost swallowed her up as she sat back, her feet unable to touch the floor. She reached into the pocket of Samson's hoodie and took out her phone, hoping that there was enough charge to ring

Beth – she didn't want to have to hunt around his luxury apartment looking for a phone charger. Hollie opened the case – good, still fifty percent charge. She took a deep breath as she saw twenty-two missed calls from Marcus and unread text messages were flashing. She tapped onto the first message from Marcus. *"I'm so sorry, where are you? Ring me back and I'll come and get you."*

Hollie deleted the message; how could he possibly think that she would want to go back to him? Why would she ever want to see him again? She scrolled down to till she read BBB, which stood for Beth Best Buddy, tapping it to read her message. *"Ring me Hollie, ASAP. Marcus has been round this morning looking for you. Are you alright? Ring me, X."*

Hollie pressed call, waiting impatiently for the ring tone.

"Hollie!" Hollie was so relieved to hear Beth's voice. "Are you alright, where are you?"

"Beth, it's so good to hear your voice. Marcus and I had a fight last night and I'm at a friend's apartment but I can't stay here. Can you come and bring me over some clothes? I literally have nothing."

"Oh Hollie, of course I'll be right over. Send me the address and I'll come and get you. Mum and Dad won't mind if you stay with us."

"Thanks, Beth. Come to the front door and I'll

buzz you in."

She picked up the piece of paper on which Samson had written the address and text it to Beth.

Hoping that there might be something edible in the fridge, she wandered into the kitchen. There were two different coffee machines on the worktop. All other appliances were discreetly hidden behind white, shiny doors. Hollie opened what she thought was the fridge, but it was the dishwasher. She tried the next handle. Success: the fridge. Her hopes dropped though when she saw three bottles of champagne, salmon canapés and a pot of olive spread. Hollie tried the next cupboard: at last, chocolate digestives. She returned to the lounge where she found the remote control to work the huge television that was mounted on the wall. She hadn't watched morning television for an awfully long time and was amazed how quickly she was distracted by the talk show guests.

The next few hours passed quickly. When the buzzer finally did go, it made her jump and even though she knew it would be Beth, her heart began to beat quickly. Still wearing Samson's hoodie, she hurried to the door, pressing the intercom button as Samson had shown her.

"Let me in!" Hollie immediately recognised Beth's voice and let her in. Seconds later, Beth was knocking at the apartment door. Hollie swung the door open and Beth stepped inside, dropping her sports bag to the floor as she looked at her friend with concern. Hollie closed the door behind her, then turned to face Beth who threw her arms around her, then stepped back to look at her properly.

"My God, what happened? Look at your face! Did Marcus do that to you?" Beth stepped forward lifting her hair away from her eye to get a proper look. "He came round to the house looking for you this morning, before you rang. I don't think he believed me when I told him I didn't know where you were." Hollie could tell Beth had lots to tell her, she was talking so fast.

"Come through to the lounge and tell me what happened," Hollie said as she brought Beth into the lounge.

"When I left my house, I spotted Marcus's car – he was parked at the end of the road. I drove past him after I turned right at the junction, then I noticed he was behind me."

The two girls sat down on the sofa, Hollie's face full of panic. "He could be outside – did he see you come into this building?"

Beth grabbed hold of her arm. "It's alright, I lost him in traffic. I kept driving in circles till he was a few cars back, then we got separated at the lights."

Hollie breathed a sigh of relief. Beth started to

look around the lounge, her jaw beginning to drop. "Wow, whose is this flat?"

"It belongs to Samson." Hollie knew Beth would need a lot more detail than that.

"Samson – why don't I know about Samson?" Beth moved closer to Hollie, not wanting to miss any small detail.

"I only met him a couple of days ago. He's moved into the apartment up the hallway from us. His parents purchased it to rent out and he's renovating it for them. They own several, this being one of them. Of course, this one is empty which is why he brought me here and said I could stay a while."

Beth still looked a little confused. "Okay, so how did you end up bumping into Samson after your fight with Marcus?"

Hollie felt embarrassed and slightly awkward for some odd reason that she needed some stranger to rescue her, but she felt less so as she started to tell Beth the story.

"Marcus walked me home from the diner last night. When we got in, we started to argue about me working at there and he said I had to give notice. We argued, I tried to leave, he hit me, I fell to the ground. I heard Samson knock on the door, then he knocked Marcus to the floor, came straight into the front room, picked me up and carried me out of there in his arms. Then he drove me here."

Beth was silent for a moment. "What a guy." She placed her hands together in front of her face, thinking for a moment.

"I think you should stay here, Hollie."

Hollie looked disappointed. "No, I want to come back with you – you're my best friend, I need you."

Beth reached over and took her hand. "You're more than welcome to come back with me, but Marcus will find you there. He's probably waiting for you now. He will stop at nothing to get to you if he knows you're there. My parents couldn't stop him. If this Samson has protected you once, he will again. I think for now you should stay here."

Hollie really wanted to go back with Beth to her parents' house. She didn't know Samson that well, certainly not well enough to be staying alone in an apartment that belonged to his parents. However, she also knew that Beth was right. Who knew what Marcus was capable of? She certainly didn't want to bring Beth's parents any stress.

"I'm just going to take a quick shower and put on some of those clean clothes you brought me. I won't be long."

She left Beth watching television and went into the bedroom, picking up the bag that Beth had brought with her from the hallway. She put it on the bed, then went into the ensuite bathroom to have a shower.

*

Beth wandered around the apartment, amazed by all the beautiful things in it. She enjoyed looking at the various art pieces and gazed for ages at the wonderful paintings hanging on the walls. Suddenly, she heard a knock at the door which then opened. She smiled at the good-looking man with big shoulders, muscles bulging out from his T-shirt, curly hair to his shoulders.

Beth walked towards him. "You must be Samson. Hollie has told me all about you."

Samson looked a little embarrassed as she looked him up and down. "And you must be Beth." He held out his hand, trying to be courteous and well-mannered. He shook her hand gently. "Where's Hollie?"

"Oh, she's in the bedroom."

Samson was holding Hollie's antibiotic prescription. He walked back down the hall where the bedroom door was open. He walked straight in but couldn't see her at first, then the bathroom door opened and Hollie stepped out wearing just a towel, her hair dripping onto her shoulders and down her skin. They both froze – Hollie felt awkward; she hadn't even heard him come home. Samson felt awful, seeing her look embarrassed and immediately turned away to face the window.

"I'm so sorry, I wouldn't have come in if I thought you were taking a shower." Samson took a few steps closer to the bed and placed her prescription beside Beth's bag of clothes. Then he backed out of the bedroom without looking at her again.

He went back down the hall to the kitchen where he put some shopping in the fridge then went in to the lounge, sitting down opposite Beth. A few minutes later, Hollie appeared, now dressed in jeans and a pretty blouse.

"Thanks for the clothes, Beth, I feel so much better now." Hollie had tied her hair up, leaving a small section down to cover the lump and bruise above her eye.

Beth got up. "I better be getting back now, Hollie. Ring me tomorrow and I'll let you know if Marcus has been round again." Beth looked over to Samson. "Bye, Samson, it was a pleasure."

Hollie followed Beth to the front door and gave her a hug. "I'll ring you tomorrow." She closed the door behind her, then went back to Samson who was still sitting in the lounge.

He was a little puzzled as only this morning she had told him she would be leaving to stay with Beth, yet she hadn't gone. She sat opposite him, perched on the end of the sofa, keeping her feet on the floor. She didn't want to tell him that the reason for not going with Beth was because Marcus would find her easily there but he'd never find her here.

"Is it still alright if I stay here? I promise it won't be long, maybe just a week."

Samson looked up at her. "I said before – stay as long as you need. I've got to go out later to meet up with my sister, then I'll go back to my place. You've got the key, just come and go as you please. I've picked up some shopping and put it in the fridge, just a few things to keep you going. I'll call in at the end of the week to see how you are, if that's alright."

Hollie smiled. "Thanks. I'd like that."

"Before I go, though, I'll cook your tea. Don't expect anything too fancy."

Hollie sat back on the sofa, feeling quite relaxed in his company. "Are you going anywhere nice tonight with your sister?"

Samson laughed. "My sister Sophia and I are close. She insists on us meeting up occasionally, sometimes with my friends, sometimes with hers. Occasionally, I choose but it's usually Sophia. Tonight, it's her friends with her venue choice."

"That sounds like a lovely thing to do. But you don't sound too impressed – is that because of where you're going or the people you're going with?"

"Sophia's friends are alright, despite her always trying to match me up with one of them. Tonight, we're going to a country and western pub for a line dancing evening."

Hollie laughed. "Oh no!" She didn't think that Samson looked the line dancing type. "I might just enjoy an evening of watching a bit of telly."

Samson stopped smiling when he began to think about the line dancing.

"What did Beth mean when she said that she would tell you tomorrow if Marcus came around looking for you again?"

Hollie looked anxious. "He was waiting outside Beth's house this morning, then tried to follow her. Beth lives with her Mum and Dad; I don't want to bring them any aggro. If he knows I'm there, he won't stop till he sees me. That's why I can't go to Beth's house."

Samson looked concerned and took out his phone. "I'm going to ring my sister and cancel tonight. If Marcus is still looking for you, I think I should stay with you." He began to scroll down his phone for Sophia's number.

"No, please don't cancel. I'm sure your sister is looking forward to it. Please, you must go. I'll feel awful if you don't."

Samson looked at Hollie; her face was a reminder of what Marcus could do. "No. I won't leave you here by yourself."

Hollie really didn't want him to let his sister down, trying to persuade him to go one last time. "I'll be fine here. I'll lock the door and won't let anyone in, I promise."

Samson didn't want to let his sister down, but he wasn't going to take a chance on leaving Hollie alone. He paused for a moment. "Why don't you come with me?"

Hollie smiled. "Really, line dancing?" She rarely went out these days. Whenever she did, there was always a consequence, so it wasn't often worth the trouble. She paused for a moment, knowing this would mean that Samson wouldn't have to let his sister down. "I'd love to."

Hollie couldn't understand why he wasn't already taking his girlfriend. He must have one – a good-looking bloke like him surely had a young lady. Maybe she had other plans tonight.

Samson smiled, pleased that was all sorted. "Are you hungry?"

Hollie hadn't eaten much since yesterday when Bob had made her a sandwich for her lunch. "Yes! I could only find chocolate biscuits earlier."

Samson walked into the kitchen. "I called into the bakery on my way back and picked us up some pasties for tea. Sorry it's nothing spectacular, but I don't really cook much."

Hollie closed her eyes briefly, and smiled.

"That sounds lovely," she called back to him, sitting back on the sofa with her legs tucked beside her. Samson returned shortly with two plates and a bottle of tomato sauce. Hollie didn't dare take the sauce, not wanting to spill anything over the furniture. He was so relaxed that he put his feet up on the coffee table. Thinking back to last night, Hollie couldn't remember him getting cross, raising his voice or losing his temper as the situation unfolded. He had been just as calm as when he was sitting in Mrs Stucky's kitchen drinking tea with her. When they had finished eating, Samson took their plates into the kitchen.

"Would you like me to wash the plates?" Hollie said, standing up, not wanting him to think she was lazy.

"No, leave it, I'll do it later." Samson looked at his watch. "We best go in twenty minutes. It's only a ten-minute drive, but Sophia will give me grief if I'm late."

"I'll go and get ready."

In the bedroom, she emptied the contents of the bag that Beth had brought on the bed, looking for something that would be suitable to wear to a country and western evening. She picked out a blue gingham checked shirt. Beth had shoved a small makeup bag in the side pocket and a hairbrush.

When Hollie came back into the lounge, Samson had showered and changed; he was leaning against the wall on the roof terrace wearing jeans and a white T-shirt. Samson looked up immediately as she joined him on the terrace. Her skin was showing through her ripped jeans, her hair was tied up in a loose ponytail with a long fringe hanging to one side over her bruised and swollen eye. He looked at her, not wanting to overstep the mark with a compliment but he couldn't help himself.

"You look beautiful." Quickly realizing how that might have sounded, he walked back inside. "Come on, let's go."

Hollie smiled, knowing he was trying to say something nice to give her confidence, despite having cuts and bruises on her face which she had tried to hide as best she could with some subtle makeup.

Samson picked up his jacket. "My truck is outside. That's the good thing about living in this street, it's permit parking only so you can always get a space. Not like Albert Street where sometimes you have to park so far away that you feel you should get a taxi home."

He opened the front door and she followed him down the stairs and outside. She looked up and down the street, feeling a little anxious being outside. Samson pulled the front door shut, then walked next to her. Suddenly, she felt relaxed, a feeling that she hadn't felt before, a feeling of being safe, that no one would hurt her while he walked beside her. Samson opened the passenger door of his truck and held out his hand to help her get in, trying to be gentleman-like. Hollie took his hand while she stepped up to get in. Seeing it in daylight, she could see the back seats were messy, cluttered mainly with tools and clothes.

Samson jumped in. "Sorry it's untidy. I wasn't expecting anyone in it. I usually just use my truck for work, carrying tools and equipment about."

Hollie moved some tools across the seat so she could fasten her seat belt.

"It's fine, really. It reminds me of my dad – he's a builder back home and his truck is like this."

Samson drove for nearly ten minutes but couldn't park outside the venue so he found a parking place much further up the street beside the river. He stopped the truck, getting out to open the door for Hollie but she wasn't used to such gentlemanly behaviour so she jumped out before he had chance to help her down.

"It's only a short walk from here." Samson looked down at her shoes; she was wearing pumps. He smiled – most girls he took out wore ridiculous shoes that they could barely walk in, usually ending in them taking them off halfway through the evening or refusing to walk anywhere at all.

They crossed the road and walked through a park. Many people were enjoying evening strolls, making the most of the light summer evening. They walked through an iron gate and out onto another busy street where they faced a big building.

"That's it. Sophia said she would meet us inside."

Inside was noisy, full of people mostly dressed in cowboy style, with big boots and cowboy hats. A live band was performing on a stage surrounded with hay bales at the far end of the bar. The dance floor in front of the stage was filled with people line dancing, all having a fabulous time. Samson spotted his sister on a long table with her friends towards the back. She had spotted him too, standing up to wave to him.

"There they are. Come on. I'll introduce you."

Hollie was feeling a little nervous of meeting new people she didn't know anything about. She felt awkward as she didn't want to answer questions about the marks on her face nor the forming friendship between her and Samson. She followed him till they reached Sophia and her friends. Sophia was already up on her feet and flung her arms around her brother. Her long curly hair was similar to his. She kissed him on the check, then quickly let go of him to look at Hollie as Samson stepped to one side.

"This is my sister, Sophia." Samson knew his sister was excited to meet Hollie and was hoping that it would only last a few minutes, then she would leave her alone.

Sophia took Hollie's arm. "Come and sit down with us. I've got you both cowboy hats."

"Great, thanks Sophia." The sarcasm in his voice made Sophia smile. "I'll just get me and Hollie a drink from the bar." He looked at Hollie. "What do you want to drink?"

"Just a soda, please." Hollie didn't want him to leave her but knew it would only be for a few minutes. Sophia led her away, sitting down next to her at the table. One of the other girls sat down on the other side of her.

"I picked up an extra hat when Samson text me to say he was bringing you."

Hollie felt awkward. "I'm sorry to intrude on your evening out with him. It was a last-minute thing."

Sophia suddenly looked embarrassed. "No, please, I didn't mean it like that. I'm so pleased he brought you along. Samson never brings a girl to any of our nights out. He always comes alone. I only ever see him with girls when we bump into each other when we're both out with our friends. He's always kept his girlfriends very separate from his family. You must be incredibly special to him since he's brought you to meet me."

"No, it's not like that at all – we're just friends." Hollie wasn't sure what Samson had told her, so she didn't want to say something different.

Sophia laughed. "I think I'm going to like you. Whatever happened to your lip?"

Hollie remembered her swollen lip was still visible to all to see.

"I cut it." Hollie desperately needed to change the subject, so she was relieved to see Samson walking back towards her.

Sophia went around the table, introducing the other girls. When Samson got back to the table, he sat on the only free seat opposite Hollie.

"Are you a student, Hollie?" Sophia continued her questioning, determined to get to know her better.

Hollie looked over to Samson, who had been forced to wear his cowboy hat. She smiled then looked back to Sophia. "Yes, I'm about to start my final year of a veterinary degree."

"Wow, that sounds amazing! You must love animals then?"

"Yes, I grew up in a small fishing village surrounded by animal farming. Since I was young, I've always wanted to be a farm vet."

"You must've studied hard at school. What a great job you'll have. However did you meet my brother?"

Hollie decided to tell her some truth now, still not knowing how much she already knew.

"Samson is renovating an apartment in the same block that I live in." Hollie didn't want to tell her much more than that for now. She looked over to Samson. The girl next to him was leaning in close to him, trying to talk to him above the sound of the music, her face close to his. He looked at Hollie, noticing that she was looking at him, and immediately smiled at her. The girl next to him gave Hollie a long stare. Samson didn't like being sat apart from Hollie – he felt like a naughty schoolboy, made to sit away from his friend. He stood up.

"Come on, Hollie, shall we give this line dancing thing a go?"

Hollie quickly got to her feet, relieved that she could escape all the questions, but not so relieved that she would show herself up on the dance floor. They joined the end of one of the lines. Samson steadied his hat.

"It can't be that difficult, let's just follow the folks in front," he said.

Hollie gave him a look of dread, but shortly after she began to enjoy dancing together. The moves were quite repetitive and she soon began to remember what steps were coming next. She looked at Samson; he, too, could remember the next steps. Sophia and her friends came to join them at the end of the line next to Hollie.

The band kept playing, song after song. Hollie loved it. Even when she occasionally turned the wrong direction, it didn't matter – she corrected herself and carried on. The evening went quickly and soon she felt hot and tired. She touched Samson's arm to get his attention.

"Do you mind if we go? I feel so tired."

"Sure. Let's go say 'bye to Sophia. I think she's at the bar."

They found Sophia chatting to some bloke at the bar.

"We're off now." Samson kissed her on the check.

She put her arm round him. "Make sure you ring me soon." She turned to Hollie. "Hollie, it really was lovely to meet you. I hope I get to see you again soon."

Hollie smiled. "It was nice to meet you too. Maybe I'll see you again?" Hollie knew that she would probably not see her again. In a few days or a week, she would have moved out of Samson's apartment, and would probably not have a reason to see him again.

She followed him through the busy bar towards the front door. There were a lot of people in the way but he seemed to snake through the crowds who moved out of the way to let him through. She found it hard to stay close behind him and within seconds he was out of sight. She thought she knew the direction of the door but she walked for several minutes, unable to find the way out. She couldn't see over people's heads, she was too short. A man beside her, holding a bottle of beer, smiled at her.

"Hey, darling, you're looking lost. Do you want to have a drink with me?"

"Not really, thank you," she replied just as she felt someone's hand grip hers. Even before turning her head, she knew it was Samson. He held her hand tight, leading her through the crowd till they got outside.

"I thought I'd lost you for a moment in there." He let go of her hand, not sure if she would want him to still be holding on to her. She smiled, wishing that he hadn't let go.

"Thanks for this evening. I didn't think I would like line dancing, but I actually really enjoyed it."

"Yeah, the evening was better than I expected, too."

They walked back towards the truck. The night was still quite warm and the sky was clear. Samson took off his hat, throwing it in the back seat of the truck.

"I'm sorry about my sister, all the questions. I don't know why she feels she needs to find out every little detail about you."

"Don't worry, it was fine. I like her."

He drove back slowly, parking his truck beside the park, opposite the apartment.

He jumped out. "Come on, I'll walk you up, make sure you get to the door – then I better get back. I've got the rest of the kitchen to fit tomorrow. Hector is coming over to give me a hand."

Hollie liked spending time with Samson; she felt comfortable with him. Would this be the last time she would see him? They got to the third floor where Hollie used her card to open the front door. She went in, then turned to Samson; he didn't follow her in but waited at the door. She paused for a moment.

"Thank you for today and all you've done for me. I'm not sure what would have happened last night if you hadn't got me out of there."

She looked straight at him as his eyes fixed on

hers. He stepped closer, placing the palm of his hand on her face. Leaning closer to her, he kissed her on the cheek. She closed her eyes. His soft touch made her think he would kiss her on the lips. He stepped back and she opened her eyes.

"I'll text you tomorrow. Now, lock the door."

He smiled, then began to walk back down the stairs. He desperately wanted to kiss her again, but didn't want to take advantage or risk her pushing him away – he didn't want to look a fool.

She closed the door and went into the bedroom. It had been a long day and she was tired.

Chapter Five

Hollie woke to the sun streaming in, forcing its way through the gaps in the shutters that she mustn't have closed properly the night before. She turned over to escape the sunlight, but it was no good; she couldn't go back to sleep. She flipped herself over again, lying comfortably for a few minutes longer. She went through a list in her head of the things she needed to do that day. Firstly, she must go and buy herself some new clothes. Beth's clothes were a perfect fit, but Hollie had more of a conservative dress code. Beth's skirts were a little too short, her tops a little too tight, and generally showed a bit more skin than Hollie liked.

She did consider for a moment whether she should go and collect her things from her and Marcus's apartment, then ruled that out immediately at the thought of a confrontation with him. Clothes and her personal possessions were not important to her anymore. There was a time when all her belongings were a priority and contributed to her decision not to walk away. She always knew their relationship would break up one day, that it could never be amicable, and they would each take what was theirs and go their separate ways.

Hollie had many items that were special to her and she knew she risked losing them. Until now, she hadn't found the courage to walk away. She got up and opened the shutters. The room was filled with glorious sunshine. What had she been waiting for? She didn't know. Maybe she was just waiting for a gentle nudge from someone. Today was to be her fresh start; her life after Marcus started now. She was determined not to rush into a new relationship and instead would concentrate on her studies.

She wandered down to the kitchen, curious to see what Samson had put in the fridge the day before. She didn't have her hopes up – after all, he seemed the type to eat out or buy ready meals with little actual cooking involved. She opened the fridge and her eyes widened as she saw the selection of food on the shelves: croissants, yoghurts, bread, cheese and fresh fruit. She felt bad for thinking he wouldn't have bought nice food. She took out a couple of croissants, made a coffee then went to sit on the balcony. The sun had warmed the cushioned seats, giving her a warm feeling as she sat down. She took a moment to adjust to the bright sun shining straight down on her, sitting back and closing her eyes to soak up the sun. It felt like a dream being here in this luxurious apartment, almost like she was on holiday. It would end soon as she remembered she was back at work tomorrow. Hollie hoped her lip swelling would have gone down a bit more by then. She knew Bob would let her work on the bar if her face didn't look any better, so she didn't have to wait on tables.

Hollie opened her eyes, thinking now of her plans for today. First, she would shop for some new clothes, then call by the university campus accommodation office and see what they had available and how soon she could move in.

The view from up here was amazing – she could see the whole city. She looked for a big church with a narrow steeple – this stood at the end of Albert Street – and wondered if Samson was there, working in his apartment. She remembered his soft touch from last night. Maybe, she thought, she was reading too much into this. It was, after all, just a goodbye kiss on the cheek. He probably did that to all the girls he knew. He did say that he would text today, but maybe he just meant that he would just text to check she was alright. She checked her phone; it was still on silent, knowing that Marcus wouldn't yet be fed up with phoning; yes, there were ten missed calls and a text message from him. Hollie tapped onto the message.

"Please call me, I'm so worried about you. I need to talk to you."

Immediately, she deleted it, not wanting to read it again. She finished her breakfast in the morning sun then returned indoors, going back to the bedroom to rummage through Beth's clothes, hoping that she might find something she would consider wearing. She chose a summer dress and a pretty cardigan. Her phone began to flash again with another message. She wondered how long Marcus would continue trying to contact her and maybe she should just message him back, telling him she didn't want to see him again and to stop calling and texting. She picked up her phone and couldn't help but smile when she saw it was a text from Samson. She sat down on the bed and began to read.

"Hey, how are you today?"

Hollie tapped back her reply quickly. *"I'm good thanks, and you?"*

She pressed send, then waited eagerly for his reply. Minutes passed as she clutched the phone in her hands; she started to wonder if he would reply at all. Suddenly, the phone flashed again, and she tapped the screen. *"Yeah good. Hector not coming out to help with kitchen today, so I'm taking the day off. Didn't know if you wanted to come for a picnic with me?"*

Hollie nearly fell off the bed with excitement. She

was smiling so much the cut on her lip was hurting her. She couldn't understand her excitement – she and Samson were merely friends but the thought of spending the day with him filled her with happiness. He was so easy going, kind, gentle and, of course, extremely good-looking.

She paused for a moment, not wanting to seem too eager. Maybe he was only offering to take her out for a picnic out of kindness, as she had had a hard time recently and he was just being nice. Thinking more about it, Hollie thought that was more likely the answer. She didn't really want to get herself back into another relationship so soon after Marcus. She needed to adjust to a life being single again, concentrating on herself for once. Hollie messaged back. *"I would love that."*

His reply came back quickly this time. *"Great, I'll pick you up in an hour."*

Hollie looked at the clock – she was still in her pyjamas. She hurried into the shower, then spent ages drying her hair. She wore it down – it had a natural curl – and with a clip she put up the fringe to stop it hanging down over her face. Beth's summer dress fitted her perfectly. Just as she picked up her cardigan, the doorbell buzzed. She hurried to open the door. Samson stood there casually in his blue jeans and T-shirt that was a little too tight around his upper arms. He smiled immediately on seeing her.

"You look amazing."

Hollie smiled back; she hadn't heard a man say nice things to her in a long time.

"Come on, my truck is outside." Hollie closed the apartment door and followed him down the stairs. He opened the front door for her, then they walked side by side till they reached the truck. He opened the door for her.

"Hey, you've given it a clean!" Hollie said as she jumped in, fastening her seat belt.

Samson grinned. "I knew you were getting into my truck today – yesterday was last minute, so I didn't have chance to have a tidy up."

Hollie glanced to the back seat, which looked clean. A wicker picnic basket sat on the back seat with a blanket beside it.

"Where are we going?" she asked.

"That's a surprise. But it's not far." Samson started truck.

Hollie couldn't remember the last time she had been on a picnic – maybe when she was a child at home, with her parents and sisters. Marcus had never taken her for a picnic. He always wanted to eat out in restaurants, go to theatres or shows, and she was always expected to dress up or wear something that was suitable to match the occasion. Often it involved meeting up with Marcus's friends or work colleagues.

Hollie looked at Samson. There was something quite simple but perfect about going for a picnic together. He must have sensed her looking at him and turned his head. They looked briefly at one another, then both looked away. The traffic was heavy, and they stopped at traffic lights regularly till they got out of the city and onto the open road, driving east of the city. Samson pulled off the main road, taking a narrow track that twisted uphill through some woods, then out into a clearing. He parked on some grass beside the track and got out, grabbing the picnic basket from the back seat. Hollie jumped down from the truck, following him down a path to a grassy area, perfect for a picnic. Hollie looked in front of her at a beautiful lake surrounded by trees. The water was perfectly still; she could see the refection of the trees in the surface. It must have been a fishing lake as she could see little coves all around it, with little wooden benches dotted along the water's edge.

Samson lay the blanket on the grass and Hollie sat down, stretching her legs in front her.

"This place is beautiful. I can't believe we're only a few miles from the city."

Samson sat next to her, placing the picnic basket on the corner of the blanket. He took out two bottles of water, passing one to Hollie.

"I hope I'm not taking you away from your work," she said taking the water from him.

"Hector called me earlier – he had to take my mum out. She really wanted to go to Hampton Court and wander through the gardens. He always puts her first, above anything. We'll finish the kitchen units tomorrow."

"He sounds like a real gentleman."

"My mum deserved someone special after spending years with my dad." Samson opened his water, taking a drink.

"Do you still see your dad?" Hollie crossed her legs under her, turning to face him. Samson's expression had changed and for the first time she saw sadness in his face. She started to wish that she had veered the conversation towards something else.

"When anyone asks about my dad, I always think of Hector. The man before was a horrible person. He was a bully who physically and emotionally tormented my mum. Sophia luckily doesn't recall many memories of him – none of the bad ones, anyway. She was only six. I was eight when my mum finally left him."

Hollie looked at him with sadness. She knew only too well what life was like to live with a controlling bully. Samson's mum must have felt trapped, with two children to worry about and protect.

"She would try to hide it from me, but I would hear and see with my own eyes what was going on. I wanted to kill him for hurting her."

Hollie couldn't imagine how an eight-year-old Samson could have stopped such a man.

"Did Hector show up?"

"No, nothing like that. One night, I heard them arguing; I could hear him raising his voice to her so I decided to go downstairs, dressed in my pyjamas. I was ready to stand up to him. After he hit her, I threw myself at him, lashing out at him. He punched me in the face and broke my jaw."

Hollie put her hands together over her mouth, shocked that a father could do such a horrible thing to their child. "I'm so sorry."

"Mum took me and Sophia to the hospital that night and we never went back. We never saw him again after that night."

"Where did you go?"

Samson looked at Hollie and smiled, reassuring her.

"At first we stayed at my gran's. That wasn't easy for my mum – Gran wasn't the easiest person to live with. A couple of months later, we moved into a one-bedroom apartment. Sophia and I shared the bedroom and Mum slept on the settee. It was small, we didn't have much money, but we were safe and together. She got herself a part-time job in a local hardware store. One day, Hector walked in, and life for her completely changed. He told me that when he saw her for the first time he knew, he knew she was the one."

Hollie felt sad that he had been through so many troubles as a child. To look at the strong, confident man he had become she would never have thought he had struggled with anything.

Samson looked at her. "I guess that's why I came for you. When I saw you in the lift that night, you behaved differently from the confident girl that you were at Mrs Stuckey's and at the diner. Later, when I heard him shouting, then a glass smashing, I knew what was coming next."

Hollie looked away, embarrassed by her own stupidity, by not walking away earlier. His mum had a reason to stay – she had her two children to think about. Hollie just had herself.

"Please don't feel awkward," he said. "I know doing the right thing isn't always the easiest thing. I knew I had to come and get you out of there. Is he still ringing?"

"Yeah, ten times last night."

"Don't worry. He'll soon get fed up with it."

She wasn't so sure. To Marcus, Hollie was the perfect accessory to fit his lifestyle. She always looked the sweet, pretty girlfriend when they went out; she did and always said the right thing around his work colleagues and friends; and his parents adored her. No, she certainly didn't think that he would let her walk away so easily.

Samson could see the sparkle and happiness that had been there earlier had now gone from her face. She sat with her arms over her knees, looking out over the lake. He wished they hadn't got into such a deep and meaningful conversation about his dad and Marcus. He wanted to do something to rekindle that smile again.

"Let's go for a swim in the lake!" Samson jumped up, holding out both his hands to pull her up off the rug.

Hollie took both his hands, allowing him to pull her up. "Are you mad? I don't have anything to wear! I only have my dress."

Samson looked at her dress, raising his eyebrows. "I have an old shirt in the truck that I use to paint in – it's clean. You can put that on if you like."

Hollie wasn't keen to wear an old shirt, but the sun was scorching down and she did really like the idea of swimming in that lake.

"Alright, I'll meet you at the water's edge." She

quickly returned to the truck and left her dress on the seat, replacing it with an old blue shirt she found in the back. She walked down to the lake in her bare feet, carefully walking over the pebbles before reaching the water. Samson left his jeans and T-shirt on the rug, meeting her at the water's edge in his shorts. There was no one else around, just the two of them. Hollie waded in slowly, getting her body used to the water until it was deep enough to swim. Samson ran, then dived in, disappearing under the water, popping up just in front of her. She splashed him and he laughed, but didn't splash her back.

"Let's swim out to those rocks." He pointed out to the middle of the lake. Hollie looked; it didn't seem too far and she was, after all, a confident swimmer.

"Alright," she said and started to swim slowly out to the rocks. Samson swam from side to side, sometimes swimming under her, sometimes just behind her but always only a couple of metres from her. She was surprised how far it was. When, finally, she reached the first rock, she was a little out of breath and she clung onto it. Samson climbed up onto the top, holding out his hand.

"Come on, I'll pull you up."

"No thanks, I'm fine in the water." She looked at him, his wet hair dripping down his face and body. He swept back his hair from his forehead then wiped the water from his eyes. He stood up, ready to dive back in. She could see his muscles as his body hit the water.

Hollie looked back to the stony beach which seemed further away than she thought. She let go of the rock and began to swim back. Halfway back, she stopped for a moment, beginning to tread water to conserve some energy. The water was lovely, but she wasn't used to swimming so far and in deep water. Samson stopped swimming too and was beside her in seconds, putting both hands on her waist. Hollie felt immediately that she didn't have to kick her legs. He was holding her up.

"You alright?" he asked.

"Yes – it's just further out than I thought. I just need a minute to catch my breath."

Hollie felt so safe in his arms once again. She could feel his arms bringing her body closer towards his, her face next to his.

He let go of her, turning his body away. "Hold on to my shoulders and we'll swim to the shore together."

She put her arms round his neck and kicked her legs behind her, but knew Samson was pulling her back across the lake. He stopped swimming when they got close enough for Hollie to put her feet on the bottom. She stood up, pleased to be back on the shore. Her shirt clung to her, revealing every inch of her body that it touched. She wrapped her hair together on one side, squeezing it tight to wring out the water. Samson stumbled over the pebbles, distracted by her, as they walked up the beach and back towards the truck where he pulled out a towel from the back, passing it to her, not able to take his eyes off her. She took it, holding it in front of her, giving him a look with raised eyes to look away.

Realising that he was staring, he immediately turned away, beginning to walk back to their picnic. Hollie dried off then put her dress back on; she scooped her hair up, wrapped it up the best that she could without a brush, securing it up with a single hairband. She walked back and sat beside him on the rug.

"You must swim here a lot."

He smiled. "Could you tell? I love it here. No-one ever comes here. On a hot day, I bring the truck up, swim across the lake, then lie in the sunshine for a while. It always feels so peaceful."

"I've never swam in a lake before. I was surprised how warm the water was."

He opened the picnic basket, pushing it towards her. She peered in: sandwiches, chocolate cake, strawberries and apples.

"That all looks lovely!" She reached in, taking out some sandwiches, and stretched out her legs so that the sun would dry them.

They ate their picnic in the glorious sunshine, enjoying each other's company in such a beautiful setting. When they had finished, Samson pushed the picnic basket off the rug, lay back, his feet hanging off the end, and placed both hands under his head. Hollie tried to lie beside him, but couldn't find anything to rest her head on.

"Rest your head here," he said, patting his stomach. She lay back across the rug with her head resting on his stomach.

"Do you date many girls?"

Samson laughed at her. She lifted her head, resting it on her hand with her elbow placed on his stomach, not caring if it hurt him; he had just laughed at her innocent question. But it didn't seem to bother him.

"Lots of my friend are girls. I often go out with girls on dates, hang out and all that – but if you want to know if I have an actual girlfriend, the answer is no. I have never really had a full-time girlfriend. I guess I've never found a girl that I have wanted to spend every day with." He put his head back on his hands.

Hollie lay back on his stomach, content with that answer. The sun dried her quickly and the brightness forced her to close her eyes. Samson kept one hand under his head; with the other, he gently swept back Hollie's hair from her face.

"I'm glad I'm here, instead of putting together kitchen units. I know I'll have to make up for lost time though, and put in a couple of longer days this week to make up for it. Are you back at the diner tomorrow?"

Hollie felt so comfortable she could have easily fallen asleep in the sunshine.

"Yes."

The thought of being back at the restaurant woke her from her relaxed moment, pushing her back towards reality.

"I have an eleven till late shift. I'm quite pleased because it will give me an opportunity in the morning to sort out some student accommodation on the university campus. I also desperately need to go shopping for some more clothes. Beth's clothes are lovely, but I need to get some clothes of my own. I need to ring my parents too, let them know about Marcus and I splitting up – of course, leaving out most of the details, else Mum will only be worried about me."

Hollie knew her mum would ask many questions and would want to know why they broke up. Her mum liked Marcus; maybe it was his masculine, charming manner that she liked or his good career prospects. Either way, she always had good things to say about him. Last Christmas, when Hollie took him back to Cornwall to meet her parents, her mum said to her: "Hold on to him! He is a charming young man." Hollie's dad was more subdued around Marcus; he wasn't convinced so easily. He, too, saw the good manners and charm, but also the self-importance. He told Hollie not to rush into anything too hastily. She knew that he could see something else, something that he didn't like. Maybe it was his fatherly intuition, but he knew something wasn't right. Hollie knew her mother would be devastated and her father relieved. She thought that now might be a good time to go back home for a week or two before the university term started. It would certainly be lovely to see all her family again. She wouldn't get another opportunity until the Christmas holidays.

Samson continued to stroke her hair, his fingers touching her face each time. She didn't want to move. His hands were big, but his touch was so gentle on her.

"I'm going out with friends tomorrow evening but I can cancel if you want me to meet you from work and drive you back home."

Hollie lifted her head, turning over to rest her hands on his chest then placing her chin on her hands.

"Please don't do that, I'll catch a bus back. The bus stops right outside the restaurant and will drop me at the end of Stanley Street."

"I was just thinking if Marcus showed up, that's all."

96

Hollie would have loved Samson to meet her from work – the thought of not seeing him tomorrow was a sad one. But she knew that she must start to get her life back on track. He couldn't chauffeur her around acting like her personal bodyguard; she knew she must carry on with her normal routine, and if Marcus showed up, she would deal with it. Hollie couldn't believe that he would hurt her in public. Maybe he would just try to persuade her to go back to him. But she knew that door was defiantly slammed shut – there was no way on this earth that she would ever go back to him.

She looked at Samson. His eyes were closed. She was unsure of his intentions. He had shown signs of affection towards her, but halted them, not allowing them to go any further. Perhaps this was what he meant by just dating different girls but not wanting a steady girlfriend. Hollie was sure that she didn't want any more emotional issues in her life: being single was a good option right now. She needed to declutter her head, and spending time with Samson wasn't helping.

They lay in the warm sun, relaxed in one another's company. Hollie sat up as the sun disappeared behind a cloud. She reached over to the corner of the rug for her cardigan. Samson too sat up, looking at his watch. It was four o'clock.

"Shall I drop you back now?" He was pulling his T-shirt over his head.

"Yes, thank you." Hollie slipped her pumps back on as he folded up the rug. "I really can't thank you enough for letting me stay your apartment. Are your parents alright with me staying there?"

Samson put the hamper and rug on the back seat of the truck, then opened the door for her.

"Yes, I've told them that you're staying for a couple of weeks."

"And are they alright with that?" She was looking for reassurance. After all, it was a gorgeous penthouse apartment that must be worth hundreds of pounds in rent each week.

"Yes, I spoke to Hector the night I took you there. He said it's fine to stay as long as you need." He started the truck. "Really, it's fine, please take your time to decide what you want to do and move out when you're ready."

Hollie turned to look at him. He knew she was looking at him so he faced her and smiled. The front of the truck had three seats and the empty seat between them seemed like a divider keeping them apart. Samson didn't hurry back; he wanted to enjoy every moment that he had with her. The drive back was short and he soon drove into Stanley Street, parking the truck outside the apartment block.

"I'll walk you up," he said, jumping out to open the door for her.

"You don't have to walk me up to the door, really, I'm fine."

He wasn't going to take no for an answer. He'd felt so close to her all day that he didn't want to say goodbye just yet.

"Please, I want to – I can sleep easy if I know you got home alright."

Hollie used the door code to open the main door and Samson walked with her until they got to the third floor. He stopped as they reached the apartment door on the top floor.

"Thanks, Hollie, for spending the day with me." He looked at her with heartfelt sadness that their day together had come to an end.

"I had a great day – the picnic, swimming with you…it was the best day I've had in ages."

"I'll ring you in a couple of days, see how you are."

"I would like that." She smiled, hoping that he would step closer to her.

"Are you sure you don't want me to pick you up from work tomorrow night?"

Hollie didn't want him to feel that she needed him only to protect her, this being the only reason to be with her.

"No, honestly, I'll be fine."

He took a step closer, taking her hand. Her heart began to race, waiting for him to learn towards her and kiss her. Samson held her hand for a moment then released it, stepping back. He smiled then turned to walk back down the stairs.

"I'll ring you."

She stood on the doorstep until he was out of sight then closed the door behind her. Perhaps he didn't want to kiss her. He had had plenty of opportunities all day, but not once did he even try.

She tried to put the idea of her and Samson out of her head. She walked up the hallway into the lounge. The excitement on entering this room, the beautiful décor, the balcony with its spectacular view over the city, she knew would never fade. How lucky the tenants who rented this apartment would be. Lying on the settee, she took out her phone, scrolling through the names until she came to 'Mum and Dad'. She tapped to call. Her mother's voice followed the ring tone.

"Hollie... Hollie is that you?"

"Hello, Mum, yes, it's Hollie. Are you and Dad both okay?"

Her mum was so pleased to hear her voice she couldn't stop talking. She had so much news that she wanted to tell Hollie that she barely stopped for breath. Hollie felt a tear run down her face. For the first time in three years, she felt homesick. If she closed her eyes while listening to her mum's voice, it was if she was sitting at home in the kitchen, listening to her mum gossip, telling her all the news. Yet here she was, all alone, worried about what the future would bring.

"How is everything with you and Marcus?"

"Yes, I was about to tell you about that, Mum. We have decided to split up."

There was a slight pause, then she could hear her mum let out a big sigh.

"I'm so sorry to hear that, Hollie. Whatever happened? Where are you staying?"

She didn't want her mum worrying about anything; she was no longer a child and she would sort this all out on her own. She knew that a few little white lies might be needed.

"We just decided that we both had different ideas about our futures and didn't really have that much in common. I'm staying with Beth for now."

Hollie paused for a moment, giving her mum enough time to digest that bit of information. Then she quickly changed the subject, not to give her mum time to start quizzing her on the finer details.

"I'm thinking of coming down in a couple of weeks before I start my term at the university in

September."

She could hear her mum's voice change suddenly, becoming excited and louder.

"Oh, really, Hollie, that will be wonderful!"

Hollie could hear her mum relaying the information to her dad who was probably trying to enjoy some peace watching the television.

"I'll ring you in a few days to confirm the dates I'll be down."

She said goodbye to a very excitable mum, who had now completely forgotten that she had just broken up with Marcus; her coming home for a visit now outshone everything else.

After making herself a snack in the kitchen, she got comfortable on the settee for the evening. She found a good novel on a bookshelf that looked interesting and she started to read the first few chapters. However, her mind was distracted by thoughts of Samson: the moment that he held her close in the middle of the lake, his face close to hers, his eyes focused solely on her. She took a deep breath – she was probably seeing something that she wanted, not what was real.

She closed the book, not having absorbed any of the storyline at all.

Chapter Six

Hollie stood at the bus-stop dressed in jeans and a yellow T-shirt with a big sunshine on the front. It was the last of Beth's tops that she had packed for her, one that she wasn't planning to wear. However, it was the only clean thing left.

The double-decker bus turned into Stanley Street and stopped at the bus stop in front of her. She quickly got on, finding an empty seat near the window. The bus was already pretty full; she put her bag on her lap so someone could sit beside her. She needed to break her journey, getting off halfway to town at the university campus. When the bus came close to her stop, she got up from her seat and pressed the button.

As she stepped off, she could feel light rain beginning to fall.

"Typical," she thought; she didn't even own a coat

anymore. She took her cardigan out from her bag and quickly put it on. The student accommodation office was only a short walk and, within minutes, she opened the door and at last got in from the rain.

The office wasn't terribly busy; there was just one other person waiting. She sat down in one of the funky armchairs while she waited her turn. The lady called her to the desk after a few minutes.

"Good morning, how can I help you?" said the lady looking up, surrounded by files spread across her desk.

"Good morning. I'm looking for student accommodation for the start of next term, sooner rather than later if possible."

The lady looked down, flicking through some paper in front of her.

"Yes, that should be alright – we still have some availability in some of our self-catering flats. Let me take some details and I'll reserve a room for you."

Hollie was relieved that they had a room for her. The lady took down her details then told her that she could move in to the flat in three weeks. At least now Hollie felt that she no longer had to rely on anyone else for somewhere to live. She could stay at Samson's for another week, then go back home to see her family, returning two weeks later ready to start back at university with her accommodation all in place. She would talk to Bob later about having a couple of weeks off; she knew he would never refuse her.

Back at the bus-stop, the rain had now eased, so she didn't feel so silly for not wearing a coat. The bus ride into town didn't take long. It became more crowded the closer it got to town, more people squeezing on at every stop. She noticed an elderly couple getting on, looking for an empty seat. She stood up immediately, waving for one of them to take her seat. The elderly lady made her way slowly towards Hollie.

"You're so kind, my dear, thank you."

A young man opposite then stood up, allowing the elderly gentleman to have a seat too. Hollie stood their shopping trolley up in front of her so it wouldn't tip over when the bus braked.

The lady looked up at Hollie. "What a lovely T-shirt you're wearing. You are indeed like a little ray of sunshine."

Hollie laughed. "Thanks, it's my friend's – she lent it to me. I didn't think it suited me much."

The bus journey continued towards the main shopping centre. As the bus began to slow down, most of the passengers began to pick up their belongings, making their way to the front. The elderly couple stood up too, reaching for the seat in front of them to steady themselves. Hollie was planning to get off at the next stop, but when she saw the couple get up, ready to get off, she could see how busy the bus was and decided to help them.

She leaned in towards the lady. "I'm getting off at this stop, too. I'll carry your trolley off the bus if you like."

The elderly lady smiled. "Oh, thank you, my husband does struggle getting it off the bus."

Hollie pulled it behind her as she made her way down the aisle, then lifted it off the bus and placed it down on the pavement. She turned to hold out her hand for them in turn to hold on to as they stepped off.

"Thank you, young lady, you have been very kind," the man said. "We hope to see you on the way back, when our trolley is heavy from all my wife's shopping." He smiled cheekily at Hollie, then took hold of the trolley with one hand and took his wife's hand with the other. Hollie smiled at them as they walked away. "What a lovely couple," she thought. "To be so content and in love at such an old age."

She crossed the road and walked into the first shop on the corner of the main high street. She needed some tops, jeans, underwear and a couple of summer dresses. She went in and out of familiar shops where she had shopped before. She wasn't one to be too adventurous – not too short, not too bright.

Strangely, though, on this occasion she did try to persuade herself to try some different colours and styles that maybe she wouldn't usually choose. Previously, Marcus's opinion would influence her even when he wasn't even there in person. She knew what he would say when she would bring home an item of clothing – he'd make a face, shaking his head if he didn't like something, then making her feel like she would look ridiculous in it. "You have to be joking if you think that you're wearing that while you're out with me," he would say to her.

Hollie felt herself almost rebelling against him as she held up quite flamboyant and brightly coloured clothing. For the first time in an exceptionally long while, she enjoyed shopping on her own, no-one to think about pleasing or displeasing. Her cheery mood was knocked down a little when she caught sight of herself in a mirror – her fringe was swept to one side so that her hair hung loosely, exposing the bruise around her eye; her lip was still visibly swollen with a cut across it. She looked away, not wanting to be reminded of past events. She tried to be positive, to think only that her future was looking good. Getting back to university with Beth, meeting up with old friends again like she used to do before Marcus. Before long, she had bought as much as she could carry. Glancing down at her watch, she could see that she had just enough time to get the bus back to the apartment, drop off her shopping, then get to work.

Back on the bus, she hoped that it wouldn't be too busy going home; she didn't know how she would manage all her bags if she had to stand. Luckily enough, the bus was almost empty, so she found a seat near the front. She checked her phone: six messages from Marcus which she immediately deleted. She had no interest in reading them because she didn't care what he had to say. She opened Samson's message from yesterday, then tapped out: "Hey, how are you?" But she immediately deleted it, then quickly put her phone back in her pocket.

*

She was pleased to get back to the apartment, laying out her new clothes on the bed, then carefully putting them into the empty wardrobe. She took out her waitressing pinafore and slipped it over her head, put her hair up but left her fringe down. Her makeup was subtle and there wasn't much that she could do to hide the wound on her lip.

During the bus ride to work, Hollie gazed out of the window, trying to think what she might tell Bob about her face. She thought about saying she fell with a glass in her hand which smashed as it hit the floor. Or maybe no one would notice.

The diner was already filling up with customers when she arrived – the rain had brought people in for a late breakfast or early lunch. She put her things downstairs, then put her head round the kitchen door.

"Hello, Bob, looks like we're going to have a busy one."

Bob looked up, relieved to see her as usual. "Can you go on the bar, Hollie?"

Sashimi and Rashmi were both in the kitchen. On seeing her, they both stopped what they were doing and came over.

"Are you alright, Hollie?" Rashmi said, looking at her lip.

Hollie smiled. "Don't fuss, I'm fine, really." She closed the kitchen door and hurried to the bar. She knew it would be busy so she wanted to get everything stocked up before the orders came flooding in. The other waitresses hurried up and down, taking orders before clipping them into the bar. Hollie concentrated so she could pour and serve as quick as possible, going from one order to the next, sometimes doing two orders together. The other waitresses liked it when she was on the bar – she was the only one that could keep the wait for drinks to only a few minutes during the busy periods. She barely had time to glance out into the restaurant but when she had the opportunity, she saw the diner was full. Bob would be flat out in the kitchen, helping Sashimi and Rashmi; they always worked so well together. Meals would come out of the kitchen, order after order, keeping customers waiting for only a short time.

For those few hours, Hollie made teas, coffees, milkshakes and every dessert off the menu multiple times, her mind focused on fast and efficient service so that the tables could be refilled. Eventually, the lunchtime rush began to ease, and the waitresses began taking it in turns to have their breaks. Hollie knew that she would be last, as she was working the evening shift. Finally, when it was her turn, Rashmi made her a sandwich which she took to the staff room in the cellar and sat down. Bob followed her a few minutes later with two mugs of coffee.

"Thank you, Bob, you didn't have to do that."

Bob sat down opposite her. "You know I'm very fond of you."

She looked at him and smiled – she was very fond of him too. He was quite a fatherly figure to her and so kind and easy to talk to about practically anything.

"And I'm very fond of you too."

"Please tell me it wasn't Marcus that did that to you."

Hollie stopped smiling. She had forgotten about the last few days: Marcus, her injuries, living somewhere new. Now Bob was bringing her back to reality. She looked away for a moment, not wanting to make eye contact with him. She couldn't bear to see his face.

Finally, she looked at him. "I can't."

His face changed to a look of sadness and concern.

"Hollie, I'm so sorry. Is there anything I can do to help? Do you need some money, somewhere to stay?"

She smiled softly at him. "Thank you, Bob, but really I'm alright. Marcus and I had an argument that got out of hand the other night. He hit me and I fell on some broken glass. Samson, a neighbour across the hall, knocked on the door when he heard shouting. He came in and took me to an empty apartment that his parents own across town."

She left out the bit about Samson thumping Marcus to get him out of the way.

"Marcus and I are over; I'm not going back to him."

Bob sat back, relaxing his shoulders, breathing out a sigh of relief.

"I'm so glad you're out of that relationship. I can't believe anyone could hurt you. What a kind neighbour you have! I'd like to meet this Samson so I can thank him myself."

She smiled, sipping her coffee. She wished Bob could meet Samson; she knew he would certainly like him. But the chances of Hollie seeing him again were slim, never mind Bob. Bob stood up.

"I'm glad you're okay. I'd better get back to the kitchen so Rashmi and Sashimi can have a break. You'll let me know, though, if I can help you in any way, won't you?"

"Yes, Bob, I will. Now, go on, get back to work."

Bob closed the door, leaving her alone. He was a lovely man; she knew he really meant what he said about helping her in any way that he could. She felt better for telling him. She wasn't one for hiding things from the people that cared about her and she knew that one small lie would turn to another. She had thought that she would feel embarrassed about telling people about what had happened between her and Marcus, but she didn't feel like that at all after telling Bob. Her feelings of foolishness at staying with someone who had anger issues were fading. A weight had been lifted just by talking to someone, without being judged or preached to, someone who listened and a kind offer of help. She switched on the radio, resting her feet on the chair in front, then leaned back to finish her coffee and relax for the remainder of her break.

When she returned to the restaurant floor, a couple of waitresses had gone home and two more had started, ready for the evening shift. She went into the kitchen.

"Do you have any specials tonight that you want me to push?"

Rashmi looked up from his salad preparation.

"We've got some roast beef left over from lunchtime – you can try to sell that if you can."

Hollie took selling the specials almost as a personal challenge, only to be celebrated if she sold every last one. Tonight would be relatively easy – roast beef wouldn't be that difficult to shift. Last week Rashmi had made a batch of spinach and green pea bake which really tested her and eventually she was defeated.

The evening rush was slow and only a few tables came in at any one time. Last orders were at nine o clock, and she was glad to hang up the 'closed' sign. As she headed back to the bar, she heard the door open. *"Can't people read,"* she thought, turning to greet them with a smile. She stopped immediately as she watched Marcus walking towards her. She froze till he got close to her.

"Please, I just want to talk. I'll sit over here quietly while I wait for you to finish." He spoke very calmly and sat down at an empty table. She didn't want him here. He'd never wanted to come to the diner before. He always just waited outside, usually across the street. She didn't want anyone to know he was here, so decided to treat him like an ordinary customer.

"I'll get you a coffee," she said then to the bar, careful not to make his coffee too hot. Her heart was racing with worry and anticipation as she headed back to his table. Gripping the cup and saucer with both hands, she placed the coffee on the table in front of him, hoping that for once he would be amicable and leave quickly and quietly after he had finished it. Samson wouldn't be coming to her rescue tonight since she had refused his offer to see her home, and he was probably having a fantastic evening out with his friends. She stepped back from Marcus's table, not wanting him to see that she was breathing quickly and shaking with fear at the thought of what could happen if she didn't do or say what he wanted.

"Please, just hear me out," he said dragging the coffee cup closer to him. "I know I've hurt you in every possible way. I'm so sorry for that. The last few days I've missed you – I need you. Please come back with me to the flat so we can talk about us."

She tried to speak quietly and softly to keep their conversation as calm as possible.

"Marcus, I don't want to go back with you. I want you to leave. It's over between us. There is nothing for us to talk about. I'll never be able to forgive you for what you have done."

He looked shocked; that obviously wasn't what he was expecting to hear. He was clearly trying to stay calm and show her that he could talk to her without losing his temper.

"I'm only asking for a few minutes of your time," he said, his voice beginning to get a little louder.

"Please, Marcus. Please accept it's over. There is nothing left for us to talk about."

Hollie could see Bob walking up the diner towards her, with Rashmi following closely behind.

"Please go, Marcus."

"Everything okay, Hollie?" Bob asked as he got closer to her

"Yes, Bob, I'm fine thank you. This is Marcus; he just popped in to say hello and now he's leaving."

Marcus stood up. "Hello, Bob."

Hollie could tell he was becoming angry and began thinking quickly how she could calm the situation.

"You don't mind if Hollie finishes a few minutes early, do you? We've got some things to sort out. Go and get your things, Hollie."

Hollie didn't want any trouble, especially here in the diner, not in front of her work friends. She looked at Bob.

"Is it okay if I get off early?"

Bob looked at Hollie, shaking his head.

"I don't think you should go home with him"

Rashmi stepped forward. "I think you should leave, mate. It's obvious that she doesn't want to go home with you."

Marcus clearly wasn't afraid of an old man and a young fellow in checked trousers. Hollie knew he was now incredibly angry. He stepped towards Rashmi.

"Who asked you to speak?" He clenched his fist, launching it in the direction of Rashmi, making contact with the side of his jaw.

"Please, no, Marcus!"

Rashmi fell back, landing on the floor next to Bob. Hollie didn't want anyone else to get hurt, especially Bob.

"Get your stuff, Hollie, we're going."

Hollie looked at Bob. "It's okay, I'll just go with him to talk to him." She really didn't want to but knew her priority was to get Marcus out of the diner as quicky as possible. She turned to Marcus. "Please calm down. I'll get my things; go and wait for me outside." She spoke as calmly and as softly as she could manage even though her body was trembling. She was scared to leave with him, but it was the only way she knew to defuse the situation. The problems it would create she would have to deal with later.

Marcus seemed to be calming down now that she had conceded to his wish to go back and talk. As she turned to go and get her belongings from downstairs, she noticed his face begin to change. Pausing for a moment, she could see the expression on his face was now one of disbelief then sheer and utter anger. Suddenly, she felt calm and her fear for her own safety, and Bob's and Rashmi's too, disappeared – Samson had walked into the diner and come up behind her.

"What's he doing here?" Marcus snarled at Hollie.

Samson walked right up to her and she felt him put his arm around her waist, slightly pulling her back away from Marcus's reach.

"Hollie is with me; I'm taking her home."

Marcus looked at Hollie in disgust.

"Are you really with him?" he said, but took a step back; he knew he was no match for Samson. He'd already been thumped by him once and knew that he wouldn't hesitate to do it again. Hollie realised that Samson was trying to make Marcus believe that they were together, trying to get Marcus to back off and leave her alone, and she played along.

"Yes, we're together. I've moved in with him." She felt Samson pull her closer still, his arm firmly around her waist. Marcus took another step back, then turned to walk towards the door.

"You can have the bitch. You're welcome to her."

Samson immediately let go of Hollie, stepping in front of her with his fist clenched, ready to punch him again. She caught hold of his other hand.

"Please, Samson, no," she said softly. Samson stopped. "Please, just let him go."

As Marcus hurried out of the diner, Samson turned to Rashmi and helped him up.

"Are you okay, mate?"

Hollie brought some ice from the kitchen to put on his face.

"So, you must be Samson," Bob said, holding out his hand. Samson shook it and smiled.

"You couldn't have timed that better."

Hollie held the ice wrapped in a towel to the side of Rashmi's face.

"I'm so sorry, this is all my fault."

Rashmi took the ice pack from her.

"Don't be silly – he sure is a nasty man. I hope that's the last you see of him."

Bob put his arm around her.

"You go and get your things and let Samson take you home." He turned to Samson. "Thank you, Samson. If you hadn't shown up when you did, I don't know how I would have stopped him taking Hollie with him. She's so lucky to have you around."

Hollie looked at Samson, feeling a little embarrassed that Bob assumed their relationship was more than what it was.

"I'll just go and get my things," she said, returning a few moments later, slipping her arms into her cardigan.

Bob put his hand on her shoulder. "I'll see you in a couple of days. Go on you two, get out of here."

Samson opened the door and she stepped on to the pavement with him. His truck was parked up the street. They walked closely, side by side.

"I thought you were out with friends this evening."

"I was," Samson replied. "But I had other things on my mind, so I wasn't really into partying."

She looked up at him as he opened the truck door for her and added, "You."

She didn't know what to say. He got into the driver's seat and started up the engine. "All I could think of was you, all evening. I just wanted to make sure you were okay."

Her heart was beating quickly once again, but this time with delight and excitement.

"I'm so glad that you did stop by. I didn't know what I was going to do. I had to get him out of the diner but knew that I was heading into a situation that

I didn't know how to get myself out of." She paused, looking over to him. "You seem to rescue me every time you see me."

He glanced quickly at her. "You best keep me around, then."

He parked the truck on the road across from the apartment.

"Come on, I'll walk you up."

"I hope that's the last I see of Marcus," she said as she jumped down from the truck.

"Me too. I think he got the message. If he thinks you are with someone else, he'll move on. But if he doesn't, don't worry – I'll deal with him. Please don't be scared of him anymore."

Hollie opened the front door and began to walk up the stairs to the third floor. Her feet were tired after such a long day. She had been looking forward to a nice bath and having a well-deserved lie-in in the morning. At the apartment door, she fumbled for the key card to open the door. At last, she found it, stepped into the apartment and turned to Samson.

"Do you want to come in for a coffee?"

Samson stood in the doorway. "No, I better not, it's getting late." He stepped closer, leaning towards her, and kissed her on the cheek. He didn't want to take advantage, nor overstep the line and scare her away, so he pulled back straight away. Hollie moved closer to him and reaching up, she kissed him, pressing her lips gently against his for several seconds before retreating.

Samson said nothing. He looked at her; he couldn't bear not kissing her again, now she had given him a taste. He leant forward, placing each hand on either side of her face, then kissed her again.

Every feeling in her body came alive. She didn't want him to let go. She reached up, putting her arms around his neck while he continued to kiss her. After a few moments, he took his hands from her face. Placing them around her body, he picked her up in his arms. She still had both arms around his neck. He stepped into the hallway, pushing the front door shut behind him with his foot, he carried her into the bedroom and lay her carefully on the bed. He took off his T-shirt, revealing abs bulging symmetrically down his chest and stomach, then began to unzip her dress. She sat up while he pulled it over her head. He lay next to her, running his fingers over her stomach, then her chest and up to her face, brushing her lips delicately with his fingertip. Leaning closer to her, he held her face gently in his hands, kissing her again. Then he placed both arms around her body, pulling her close to him so their skin was touching. Hollie's face rested on the pillow, her body squashed up against his. He held her tight. She waited for him to run his hands over her body or even remove her underwear like most men would have done, but he didn't. She had felt the passion between them; he must have felt it too, so she was puzzled why he had stopped. Maybe he didn't find her that attractive. After all, he had probably slept with loads of beautiful women with perfect bodies. Maybe after seeing hers in the flesh, he was put off at the last moment. She lifted her head of the pillow and looked at him.

"Why did you stop?

Samson swept her hair back from her face, gently stroking the bruise over her eye, then kissed her on the lips.

"Being here with you, the first night I brought you back here, I slept on the floor next to you because I couldn't bear to be too far away from you. All I wanted to do was to lie in the bed next to you and hold you in my arms. You're the most beautiful girl I've ever met and I don't want to do anything to scare you or make you feel like you have to do anything you don't want to."

She kissed him. "But I do want to."

He ran his thumb over her lip while holding her face in his hand.

"I want it to be different with you. It feels different. You are different to other girls I've met. I don't want to just go to bed with you and then go our separate ways in the morning till we bump awkwardly into one another again."

Hollie lay her head next to his chest. He turned his body towards hers, putting his arms around her, and held her firmly in his arms. She had never known a man who had got her into the bedroom and hadn't wanted sex with her at the first opportunity. This last year with Marcus, sex had been an activity that happened in the bedroom, always on his terms. There was no passion, no dramatic feeling, just a pleasing finale from Marcus indicated with a kiss on the cheek before he turned over to go to sleep.

She closed her eyes, knowing that this was going to be the start of something special. Samson was no ordinary man.

Chapter Seven

Hollie opened her eyes, her face on the pillow, facing towards the window. She could feel Samson's arm wrapped around her waist, his hand tucked underneath her. She could hear his breathing, his head just above hers. She reflected on the night before, unintentionally stroking his arm. She had spent the night with a man that hadn't tried to have sex with her, a man who hadn't let go of her all night, a man that was practically a stranger but who she felt so comfortable and safe, and who made her feel like no-one else ever had.

She noticed his breathing pattern had changed and knew he had woken. He lifted his head off the pillow and kissed her on the cheek. She turned over to face him. Pulling the duvet further up around her, she remembered that she was still only wearing her underwear from the night before.

"Hey, I slept so well."

Samson turned on to his back. "Me too – you're like a little hot water bottle."

"Do you mind if I take a shower in a bit? I don't mind if you want to go first though," she said, hoping that he would. She didn't want to get out of bed and walk to the bathroom in just her underwear, not in daylight, for him to see every inch of her body.

He laughed; he knew that she wanted him to go first so she could get some clothes on.

"No, it's fine really, you go first."

She wriggled under the covers, then sat on the side of the bed with part of the duvet wrapped around her. He didn't want her to feel uncomfortable, so he got up.

"On second thoughts, I'll go first"

Hollie waited till he had disappeared into the bathroom then quickly got a T-shirt on. She walked over to the window, opening the slats on the shutters and allowing the sunshine into the room. She went back to sit on the bed and waited for Samson to come out. Minutes later, he emerged from the bathroom, dressed in jeans and T-shirt, his wet curly hair dripping on his shoulders.

"I'll go and make you a coffee. Are you hungry?"

"Just coffee will be lovely, thank you."

He left Hollie to get up as he knew she wouldn't

want him looking at her half-naked body walking across the room. After her shower, she put on one of the new outfits that she had bought the previous day. It had looked so good on the hanger, but now she wasn't so sure. She looked in the mirror: the sky-blue skirt that buttoned down the front wasn't as long as she would normally wear – it came inches above her knees. She put on the short blue cardigan over a white blouse, trying to cover up a little. After a quick look in the mirror, she went to find Samson.

The fresh smell of coffee lifted her mood, making her smile as she walked into the lounge. He looked up straight away.

"Wow, you look beautiful."

Hollie wasn't used to such nice compliment and she felt a little embarrassed. Anyway, he probably complimented most of the girls he saw in the same way.

He passed her a mug of hot coffee.

"One of my friends, Mason, is having a pool party this afternoon and I'm planning to go. Do you want to come with me?"

Hollie frowned. "I'm not sure." The thought of socialising with a group of strangers wasn't that appealing. He took his coffee mug back to the kitchen.

"We don't have to go; we can do something else. What would you like to do?"

She did want to spend the day with him and wanted to do something that he wanted to do. Maybe it would be fun.

"Alright, I'll go with you."

He smiled. "Great! My sister will be there too. Mason's sister is good friends with Sophia. I know she'd love to see you again." He picked up his keys from the coffee table. "I need to go out for a couple of hours – I have to collect some wood from the warehouse. I'll be back in two hours to pick you up. Are you going to be alright?"

Hollie smiled. "Yes, I'll be fine. I may sit out on the balcony and catch some sun."

"Okay, if you're sure. I won't be long." Samson walked over to her, touched the side of her face with his hand, then gently kissed her on the lips. She almost dropped her coffee – just one kiss sent a wave of passion through her body. She gripped her mug with both hands. He walked out of the room and then she heard the front door close behind him.

She took a deep breath. Was this moving too quickly for her? She sat on the settee, stretching out her legs in front of her. She looked around at the beautiful apartment; it would be sad to move into university accommodation after staying in five-star luxury. She relaxed for a couple of hours and had almost fallen asleep when she heard the front door buzzer. Knowing it was Samson, who'd come to pick her up, she slipped on her pumps and left the apartment.

Outside, he opened the truck door for her and she jumped in.

"It's only a ten-minute drive. We don't have to stay long if you get fed up."

Hollie wasn't sure what his friends would think of her. She had convinced herself, though, that she wasn't the usual type of girl that Samson might date.

He glanced over to her. "You look nervous."

She gave him a smile.

"Please don't be. You look amazing."

Hollie wasn't sure if he was just saying that to help her relax.

Once they had reached their destination, Samson parked opposite a driveway where the security gate had been left open. He caught hold of her hand and held it tight. They walked up a long drive to an impressive, large house surrounded by perfectly lawned gardens. He led her around the side of the house, under an archway of roses and plants and out on to a terraced lawn leading to a swimming pool and patio area, where music was blasting from the speakers in each corner. There must have been three or four hundred people, either sitting on the lawn or around the pool. Samson spotted Mason and headed towards him, still holding Hollie's hand.

"Mason's parents have gone away for a few days," he told her. "I can't believe they trust him with all this."

When Mason saw Samson, he immediately walked over to meet him. A big smile confirmed these two were great friends.

"Hey, mate, I'm so glad you could make it." Mason put his hand out to shake Samson's, then turned his attention to Hollie. "Who is this pretty lady?" He took hold of her hand then lowered his head to gently kiss it.

"And what are you doing with Samson?" he asked, releasing her hand and smiling.

Samson laughed. "Back off, mate. Where's Becky? Has she finally dumped you?"

Mason's face changed to a concerned expression on hearing his girlfriend's name.

"Not yet, but I'm sure she's watching me from somewhere."

Samson glanced over to the other side of the pool. "There's Sophia," he said, and squeezed Hollie's hand. "Let go and say hello."

Sophia had already spotted them and began to walk towards them. Hollie was pleased to see a friendly face. Sophia flung her arms around her, giving her a peck on the check. Hollie was used to this sort of display of affection as Beth always hugged and kissed her every time they greeted or parted.

"Hollie, I'm so pleased to see you again. Bloody hell, I don't think my brother has ever taken a girl on a second date."

Sophia stood on tip toes to kiss Samson on the cheek.

"You should have told me that you were bringing Hollie. You know that Candice is here." Sophia turned to Hollie, not wanting to be rude by leaving her out of the conversation. "Candice is a friend of a friend of mine, who is only here because she thought Samson would be here. He made out with her about a year ago. My brother never returned any of her calls, nor has he spoken to her since, but she still tries to bump into him hoping that he will talk to her. Sorry, Hollie, my brother is a bit of an arse at times."

Samson looked at Sophia. "Don't be silly, that was over a year ago. Nobody holds a torch for someone for that long," he said and looked sternly at Sophia, indicating for her to stop talking.

"That's because you have never fallen in love with anyone, my darling brother."

Samson let go of Hollie's hand. "I'll just go and get us a drink," he said, and looked at Sophia. "Don't say anything else while I'm gone."

As Samson walked towards the house, Sophia stepped closer to Hollie.

"If it's any consolation, Samson never sees a girl twice and this is the second time I've seen you, so I rather think my brother quite likes you."

Hollie smiled at her. She could tell that she adored her big brother, but also liked to snitch on him — maybe this was a continuation from when they were children. Hollie knew what it was like to have older siblings, often being told what to do, or what not to do, so it was always good to turn the tables.

Samson returned with three drinks. Sophia took a large mouthful of hers.

"I think they forgot to put any wine in this spritzer."

Samson handed Hollie a glass then put his hand round her waist, stepping closer to her.

"Don't take any notice of my sister."

A small group of people walked over to them and some of the girls in the group exchanged kisses with Sophia. One of the men came over to Samson, keen to shake his hand.

"Hey mate, good to see you."

Samson shook his hand. "You too, mate."

Hollie could tell that this was another one of Samson's good friends, from the body language between them and the fact that they laughed at one another. He then turned to Hollie, greeting her with a kind smile. She thought she recognised him from the diner when Samson had eaten there a few days ago.

"You must be Hollie. I've heard lots of good things about you."

Samson quickly interrupted. "This is Noah. He likes to think he's my best mate."

"I'm only here because I was curious to meet you. Samson left a damn good party last night because he wanted to see you. In all the years I've known him, he's never put a woman first, so I had to come meet you."

"Take no notice, Hollie, he's just teasing."

"Hollie," Sophia called, "come and meet the girls."

Hollie walked over to Sophia, leaving Samson talking to Noah.

Sophia grabbed hold of Hollie's arm, pushing her in view of her friends.

"This is Mildred, Ronnie and Candice."

Hollie smiled politely at all three who were dressed like models with immaculate makeup and hair that must have taken hours to achieve. They all looked beautiful. Hollie suddenly felt under-dressed; she felt like she should be collecting glasses and serving the drinks. Sophia linked her arm, turning away from the other girls to talk to her. Hollie could hear them whispering to one another as Sophia chatted.

"She looks like a librarian," Mildred whispered.

"Why is he seeing her again? He never takes a girl on a second date."

Hollie tried to block their voices out and ignore their remarks. She concentrated on what Sophia was asking her.

"Sorry, Sophia, what did you say?"

"I said, I can't believe no-one is in the pool. Last time Mason through a pool party, everyone jumped in. We were in the middle of a heatwave, mind you. Did you know that Samson loves to swim?"

"Yes, he's a good swimmer. He took me to swim in the lake a couple of days ago."

Sophia looked surprised, then she smiled.

"That doesn't sound like my brother; he usually swims alone."

The other girls stopped chattering and began to eavesdrop on their conversation.

"I'm so glad he met you. He has never taken to a girl before. You must come round and meet our parents. It's Hector's, our dad, birthday tomorrow.

They'd love to meet you. Samson must bring you with him."

Hollie felt Samson catch hold of her hand.

"I hope Sophia hasn't been feeding you lies about me."

She turned around to smile at him. He looked pleased to be back by her side again.

"Sophia was just telling me that it's Hector's birthday tomorrow."

She was suddenly interrupted by screaming coming from the two girls standing close to them. Mildred was shouting repeatedly: "Candice can't swim, Candice can't swim!" and pointing towards the pool. Samson was the first to react. He let go of Hollie's hand and ran towards the pool, diving straight in. Candice hadn't yet surfaced when Samson grabbed her body, dragging her to the side, lifting her in his arms to carry her up the steps. He lay her gently on the grass beside the pool where she immediately started to spit out water. Gently, he rolled her on to her side. Her friends gathered around her, watching hysterically.

Samson got to his feet.

"She'll be okay." His clothes were drenched. Mason came running over.

"Well done mate, thanks for your quick reaction."

People started clapping as Mason led him towards the house. He looked around for Hollie. There were a lot more people who had now came out of the house to see what all the commotion was about. Samson went in to get some dry clothes. When he returned, he found Hollie and Sophia sitting together on a grass bank.

Sophia looked at Samson sternly.

"You do realize that she did that on purpose, just to get your attention. She knew you would jump in after her."

Samson looked confused; he didn't know how his sister had come up with that idea.

"Candice is telling everyone that you're her hero for saving her life. Honestly, Samson, you're such a clown sometimes."

He looked at Hollie who was looking in the other direction.

"I don't know what you would have wanted me to do."

Hollie turned to face him. "I want to go."

Samson still had no idea what he had done wrong for both the girls to be so cross with him.

"Well done, brother," Sophia said tapping him on the back. "I'll talk to you later." She turned to Hollie and gave her a kiss on the cheek. "Sorry for my idiot brother – jumping into the pool to rescue a girl that hadn't taken her eyes off him the entire time he's been here." Sophia didn't confirm when or if she might see her again as she could see that Hollie was annoyed.

Hollie began walking towards the driveway and back to the truck. Samson followed her, still bewildered by her hostile reaction to him. He opened the truck door for her.

"Why are you so annoyed with me?"

Hollie got in, impatiently wanting him to turn on the engine.

"Do you always save damsels in distress? That girl couldn't take her eyes of you the entire time we were there and she fell into that pool knowing that you would jump in to rescue her." Hollie didn't like the words that were coming out of her mouth; she sounded like a jealous girlfriend and didn't like that feeling at all.

"I overheard some of the other girls saying that you usually sleep with a girl, then never date her again. Is that what happened with Candice?"

Samson started to drive.

"I've no idea why you are so cross with me. If it's about Candice, I didn't know she would be there today. I went out with her, just once, about a year ago, but she wasn't for me. I have been out with lots of girls since then. I presumed that she had gone out with someone else after me. Please, I refuse to argue with you. I'm sorry for whatever I've done to upset you."

Samson continued to drive. Hollie turned to face him; he looked sad. She knew her jealousy was making a dent in their new friendship. The thought of him diving into that pool, carrying out a girl in his arms who still held a torch for him, made Hollie feel sad and she found it difficult to simmer her jealousy. She suddenly realised that she felt more for him than she wanted to.

In silence, Samson drove on. He parked the opposite the apartment but made no move to get out. Hollie reached for the door handle.

"I'm sorry, but I don't think I'm ready to jump into a relationship again, it's too soon. You are a good-looking man, you can have any girl, I think that was obvious at the party today. I don't think I'm your type of girl." She stepped down from the truck. "I'll be out of your apartment in a couple of days."

Samson turned to face her.

"Please don't walk away like this."

She gave him one last smile, then closed the door. He leaned forward, resting his head and hands on the steering wheel for a moment. He couldn't believe how he had lost her, after only just finding the best girl he had ever met.

Hollie closed the apartment door and collapsed on the settee. She put her hands over her face, lying silently, hiding from the day's events. Had she done the right thing? Had she been too hasty? She went out onto the balcony to enjoy the evening sunset. She looked over the city, peering down towards the road – Samson's truck had gone. She sat down, remembering how he had held her in his arms all night. How he never went too far from her in case she needed him. Now he was gone, and she felt an empty feeling in her stomach.

Chapter Eight

It wasn't the rain lashing down on the bedroom window that woke her, but the vibration of her phone sitting on the dressing table across the room. Hollie threw the duvet off, stumbling with her eyes shut, guided by the sound. She opened her eyes briefly to see who the caller might be. It was Bob, so she slid her finger across the phone.

"Hello, Bob, are you alright?"

"Hello, Hollie, sorry to bother you on your day off, but would you be able to come in for a few hours over lunchtime?"

She would have liked to have said that she had an exciting day planned, but apart from flicking through the telly channels, she didn't.

"Yes, that's fine Bob. I'll see you in a bit."

She thought that maybe working would be a distraction. She still hadn't been able to shake Samson from her mind. The thought of not seeing him again was becoming harder to bear. Now more awake, she looked at her phone to see if he had sent a text. Nothing. She was starting to feel like an overdramatic teenager having a tantrum. Really, he'd done nothing, apart from having a laddish reputation, only dating girls once, then not seeing them again. But he hadn't been this way with Hollie – almost the opposite. She didn't want to dwell on it any longer. She got up, got ready for work and left for the diner as quickly as possible.

The rain was pouring down as she walked to the bus-stop. On her previous shopping trip in the sunshine, she had failed to purchase an umbrella, so now she boarded the busy bus drenched from the rain. She found an empty seat at the back and checked her phone once again. Beth had text her: *"How are you, hun, must catch up soon, text me x"*

Hollie put her phone away, looking out of the window. The weather reflected her mood. People were rushing along the pavements, trying to avoid clashing umbrellas, hurrying past one another.

She walked into the restaurant, rain running down her face, wet footprints trailing on the floor behind her as she walked towards the cellar door.

"I'll make you a coffee, Hollie," Bob called out from the kitchen when he saw her.

She had packed her pinafore dress in her bag, so it was nice to have something dry to put on. She tried to redo her hair, but it was no good so she just scrunched it up into a bun. At least it was off her shoulders.

"Thanks, Bob, I really need this." She picked up the mug he had left for her just inside the kitchen door.

"Thanks for coming in. Tilly's gone off sick. Did you have a nice day off? How is Samson?" Bob smiled, hoping for some chat about her and Samson's day together. She looked away, picking up the lunchtime menus waiting to go out onto the tables.

"Oh Hollie, please tell me you haven't fallen out."

She looked across the kitchen to Bob. He stopped chopping the vegetables, looking at her with sadness in his eyes.

"I don't know; he's so popular with other girls, good-looking, such a gentleman." She paused. "I don't think I'm ready, so I pushed him away."

"Do you not think you deserve such a man? Hollie, you are the sweetest, kindest girl I know. You're perfect for each other."

"I don't want to talk about it, Bob. It's done now." She picked up the menus, took them into the diner, and started to get ready for the lunch service.

During lunch, she tried to keep busy, rushing

around and chatting to customers in between serving. She always introduced herself as their waitress before she took their order – she felt it made it more personal if the customer knew her by her first name.

After dropping off some dirty plates in the kitchen, she glanced towards the front door. An elderly lady with a stick was shuffling her feet forward, making her way away down the diner. She was accompanied by Samson who took hold of her arm to steady her.

"Mrs Stuckey!" Hollie called out. She hurried towards her, a smile beaming from her face.

Her stick in one hand and holding on to Samson with the other, Mrs Stuckey smiled back at Hollie.

"You brought Mrs Stuckey in to see me," Hollie said, looking at Samson.

He smiled at her.

"Yes, I'm just dropping her off with you for a bit. I've got something to do just round the corner. I'll pick her up in an hour and take her back."

Hollie didn't know what to say; she looked at him with delight in her eyes, thinking about how he had come back to see her.

"Aren't you staying?"

Samson helped Mrs Stuckey sit down at a nearby table.

"No, I thought I would leave you girls to chat. I'll be back later."

He placed Mrs Stuckey's stick next to her. The old lady caught hold of his arm.

"Thank you, Samson, you are a good boy."

He put his hand over the old lady's hands which were clasped together on the table. Then, looking at Hollie, he smiled before heading towards the door.

"I'll go and get you a coffee, Mrs Stuckey. I'm due for a break now."

The diner had quietened off and Bob was grinning from ear to ear when she returned to see if she could take her break and sit with Mrs Stuckey.

"Was that Samson I just saw?"

She ignored him on purpose. She placed two cups under the coffee machine. Bob placed the two saucers on a tray and put them on the counter for her.

"He can't stay away from you, can he?"

Hollie hurried back with the tray, sitting down opposite Mrs Stuckey who reached over to hold her hand.

"Oh, my dear, let me look at you. You must have lots to tell me. Samson tells me you have left Marcus and have moved into a new apartment across town."

Hollie smiled at the old lady; it was so nice to see

her. She had thought that she would never see her again, as she knew she could never return to her old apartment again.

"Yes, Marcus and I broke up." She didn't think it was necessary to give too much information as she didn't want to worry her.

"I've missed you popping in to see me, my dear. Samson has been calling in every day to check on me, but I've missed our little chats. He's such a nice boy." She leaned a little closer. "Is that a bruise over your eye?"

Hollie tried to fumble with her hairband to release a little hair to hide it.

"Is that why you left him?" Mrs Stuckey squeezed her hand from across the table. "I know it couldn't have been that Samson, not the way he looks at you. My Stan used to look at me that way." The old lady took a deep breath, remembering for a moment those happy days. "It's a look of complete and utter love and devotion. I don't think there is anything that boy wouldn't do for you."

Hollie, now feeling quite embarrassed, took a mouthful of her coffee and smiled.

"Don't be silly, Mrs Stuckey, it's not like that at all."

Despite being pleased to see Mrs Stuckey, she was also happy that she'd had the chance to see

Samson again.

"So, tell me," Hollie said. "I hope you've not been overdoing things. Have you rung that cleaner that we were talking about last week?"

Mrs Stuckey leaned back in the chair.

"You do fuss too much, Hollie, but yes, I did ring her yesterday. She's coming round to see me later to talk about some of the things that I need help with. I must admit that these days I'm finding the most basic tasks more difficult than I did before."

"Good, I'm pleased to hear it. You must accept more help. Old age comes to us all."

Mrs Stuckey barely drank her coffee but she kept hold of Hollie's hand for the entire hour, passing on all the news of things that had gone on over the past week. It hardly seemed that an hour had passed when Hollie looked up to see Samson walk through the door.

"My handsome chauffeur is here."

Samson tried not to look at Hollie as he walked towards them.

"You ready?" he asked, lifting up Mrs Stuckey's stick which had fallen on the floor and placing it in her hand.

"Have I got to get up into that truck again? You might have to lift me in this time, young man."

Samson held out his arm for her to hold.

"It will be a pleasure."

Mrs Stuckey turned to Hollie.

"It was lovely to see you again, my dear." She stood up then reached forward to tightly hold Hollie's hand once more for a moment. Sadness flooded Hollie's face; she didn't know when she would see her dear old friend again. Suddenly her throat felt blocked. She didn't want to say goodbye.

Hollie looked at Samson gratefully.

"Thank you for bringing her down to see me; that was so kind of you."

He smiled at her; she looked sad and he didn't like to see her like that. She kept eye contact with him – she didn't want him to go just yet, but nor did she want to ask him to stay. There was a pause where neither one of them wanted to look away.

"Shall I stop by and see you later, after I've taken Mrs Stuckey home?"

Hollie let out a sigh of relief inside, knowing that he still wanted to see her again.

"I thought you were going to your dad's birthday party this evening? I don't want you to miss that. Maybe tomorrow?"

He'd forgotten the family birthday for a minute.

"Why don't you come with me? My parents would love to meet you. Sophia's already told them all about you."

"Really?" Hollie had found her smile again. "Yes, I'd love to."

"I'll pick you up at six."

She was so pleased that he hadn't given up on her so easily.

"See you at six then."

Mrs Stuckey gave Hollie a cheeky grin, then she caught hold tightly of Samson's arm as he walked her slowly to the door, helping her over the step and onto the pavement.

Hollie hurried back to the kitchen, looking for Bob. He was finishing the washing-up with Rushti.

"Do you still me to stay, or is it alright if I get off?" Hollie was already undoing her apron strings.

"Yes, of course, you finish up, Hollie. Thanks for coming in at such short notice. I can always rely on you. With a smile like that across your face, I think I know who you might be seeing later."

She didn't reply and was already halfway down to the cellar to get her things. Minutes later, she was out in the street, walking towards the bus-stop in the rain. Despite getting drenched for the second time that day, her excitement at seeing Samson again couldn't be quashed in any way.

Immediately she walked into the apartment, she ran herself a hot bath. Opening the wardrobe, taking out various items of clothing, she tried to decide which outfit she felt would be appropriate for a family occasion. Her final choice was a white strappy skater dress. She wore her hair down, the ends curling over her shoulders. She was ready a few minutes early, so sat on her bed admiring the view from the open shutters. The sound of the buzzer made her jump despite eagerly awaiting the sound. She slipped on her comfy pumps, walking quickly up the hallway to open the door.

Samson stood in the doorway, dressed in his jeans, a blue shirt and jacket. She wasn't sure if she was a little overdressed. Seeing Samson's wet hair, it was obvious that it was still raining. Maybe, she thought, something warmer might have been a better choice; still, there was no time to start changing now.

"Wow, you look stunning." Samson realised he was staring too long at her and quickly held the door open for her. "Come on, let's go."

He walked beside her down the stairs and out into the street. As soon as they got outside, he took off his jacket, putting it round her shoulders. She looked up at him – no man had ever done that for her before.

"Thanks," she said, slipping her arms into his

jacket. "I'm so sorry for yesterday."

Samson interrupted her.

"No, please don't apologise. I know I don't have a good reputation when it comes to girls." He opened the truck door, offering his hand to help her up. "I don't know why but usually when I go out with a girl, I never seem to have any connection with them to want to see them again, so I move on to the next. The first date is always exciting but then the next day, nothing." Samson started the engine and began to drive. "Until I met you. I have no idea why, but you're different to other girls I know and I do know that I want to see you every day."

She looked across at him and smiled. There certainly was something that was making her want to see him every day too.

The journey to his parents' house only took ten minutes. Samson turned into a private road, parking near the top. He got out and opened the truck door for her. He placed his hands around her waist as she put hers on his shoulders. Carefully, he lifted her down till her feet were on the ground, his face close to hers. He let go, moving back, not sure if he should have kissed her but not wanting to do so uninvited.

Hollie looked up the driveway. Lanterns were staggered on both sides of the driveway and the rain, at last, had stopped. Now she began to feel nervous.

"Come on, you'll like my parents." Samson could see that she was feeling a little worried, so he caught hold of her hand. She felt a calm wave rush over her body when he gripped her hand in his. As they walked further up the drive, she soon saw that the big fir trees at the top were hiding a large, beautiful chalet-style house, only visible at the very top of the driveway. The garden was full of pretty flowers, with fruit trees dotted around the lawn. Samson paused at the front door, ringing the bell, then pulling Hollie closer to him.

The door opened to reveal a middle-aged, well-dressed gentleman. As soon as he saw them both, a charming smile appeared, which made Hollie relax.

"Happy Birthday, Dad!" Samson said. "This is Hollie."

"What a pleasure it is for me to meet you, Hollie, please do come in." Hector stood back, waiting for them to step into the hallway. He learned forward, kissing Hollie on the cheek. "Thank you so much for coming." Then, turning to Samson, he threw his arm round him. "It's always good to see you, son. Come on, your mother is fussing in the kitchen. She's waiting for you. Uncle Mick and Auntie Gemma are in the garden."

Samson, still holding Hollie's hand tightly, led her up the hallway and into the kitchen. A beautiful lady with long brown curly hair was pouring wine into glasses on a tray. Her face lit up with joy as soon as she saw them both. Immediately, she stopped what she was doing, standing still for a moment just to look at them both together. She knew from her son's face how happy he was having Hollie with him.

"It's wonderful that you're both here!" She stepped closer, giving Hollie a girly kiss on the cheek. Strangely, Hollie felt a warm, motherly feeling from her – the sort of feeling that she would get from being with her own mother.

"It's so lovely to meet you," she said to Hollie then looked at Samson. "Come here and give your mother a hug."

He went closer to her and put his arms around her.

"Are you alright? Do you need a hand with anything?"

"No, everything is fine. You can go into the garden and check Uncle Mick is behaving."

Samson looked at her.

"I hope you've not let him drink too much – we don't want to be listening to his stories all night."

He caught hold of Hollie's hand, leading her out through the kitchen patio doors and onto a large, paved area with table and chairs. There were more than thirty people standing around chatting. A man was laughing loudly while holding a pint glass, sitting with a group near the swimming pool. Hollie instinctively knew that he was Uncle Mick.

Uncle Mick got up, making a beeline for them as soon as he spotted Samson.

"This is Uncle Mick," Samson told Hollie. "Not much to tell you other than he is always the loudest at any family party – oh, and he always talks a load of crap."

Uncle Mick laughed. "This is an honour, Hollie. Samson never brings a girl to a family party." He reached forward, taking her hand to kiss it.

Samson's mum came over with a tray of drinks.

"Don't embarrass my boy, Mick, else you'll have me to answer to. Orange juice or wine, Hollie?"

Hollie took an orange juice off the tray, giving her a good excuse to take her hand back from Uncle Mick.

"Don't take any notice, Hollie. Samson will throw him in the pool if he gets out of hand."

Uncle Mick laughed. "Yeah, I might shut up now as he's done that before."

An excitable scream came from the house, causing Hollie to look around. The scream got louder then revealed its maker: Sophia leaped out of the patio doors and came running toward Hollie.

"You're here, you're here, I can't believe it!" Sophia threw her arms around Hollie. "I'm so pleased you came." She looked at Samson. "Must have done something right for a change, bro."

She turned to Uncle Mick, giving him a quick peck on the check, not wanting to get into any conversation with him, then turned her attentions back to Hollie.

"I love your dress, it's gorgeous. We must go shopping one day; you have such lovely taste in clothes."

Hollie smiled. Sophia was so excitable, it was infectious. She couldn't do anything but return a huge smile.

"I better go and find Dad, wish him happy birthday and all that." Sophia stood on tiptoes to kiss Samson on the cheek. "I'm so thrilled you got Hollie to come." She disappeared into the house to find Hector.

Samson took the opportunity to take Hollie down the garden, briefly introducing her to some family and friends, heading towards the summer house nestled in a cluster of trees in the corner of the garden. They both sat on a wooden bench next to it, Samson still holding tightly onto her hand.

"What a beautiful garden your parents have. The summer house is gorgeous. They must spend a lot of time sitting right here."

Samson stretched out his legs, leaning back. He was enjoying this moment being alone with her, looking down at her small hand entwined in his.

"Hector loves this garden. He spends a lot of time out here. Mum wants him to get a gardener, but he says he's not ready yet. He won't give in to the fact that he is getting older and should be slowing down." He paused for a moment, looking up at the house where he could see Hector talking to Sophia. "He had a mini heart attack last year. Mum is so scared of losing him that she doesn't want him to do anything. The problem with Hector is there is nothing wrong with his head. He still thinks he is a young man. He still comes up with ideas and plans for the business that he wants to implement himself. He isn't ready to apply the brakes just yet."

"I guess it must be difficult to stop something you love doing," Hollie said and could tell that Samson found it difficult to help his mum find a way to convince Hector to slow down.

"I do most of the work when we are renovating an apartment, but he still likes to get involved. I've been trying to convince him to take on someone else to help me so he can step back, but I can't convince him." Samson sat up, turning to Hollie. "Come on, let's go back to the house. Mum was so keen to meet you when I told her that you were coming."

They walked slowly, close to one another, back up the garden towards the house.

"Is it true that you've never brought a girl back home to meet your family? I just can't believe that you've never had a steady girlfriend."

Samson laughed at her. "What's so hard to believe? I've just always kept the two separate. I know it sounds crazy, but I've never really found someone that I wanted them to meet."

He stopped, still holding on tightly to her hand. He faced her, leaning forward and placing the palm of his hand on the side of her face. Before he had chance to move any closer, they heard Uncle Mick shout from the house.

"Come on, you two, your mother says the food is ready."

Samson returned his attention to Hollie, still with his hand on her face.

"I guess we should get back."

He led her back up the garden to the house. His mother had obviously gone to a lot of trouble preparing a buffet which was spread over the table. She handed them each a plate as they stepped into the kitchen.

"Help yourself, you two."

Hollie remembered that she was wearing a white

dress, so decided to choose the food she put on her plate carefully. Samson led her into a large lounge, where they sat on a settee in the corner. Samson's mum spotted them a few minutes later; coming over, she sat in the armchair close to them. Hollie felt relaxed in her company, not at all like her previous relationship where she would try to say the right answers that would have been expected from her.

"Samson didn't tell me where you two met."

Hollie looked at Samson.

"Samson moved into an apartment on the same floor that I used to live in. We met in the hallway."

Samson didn't want Hollie to stumble through trying to explain herself or how they came to be together, so he continued.

"Hollie had to move out quickly, so she's staying in the penthouse apartment on Stanley Street. Did Dad tell you?"

His mum smiled. "Yes, I think he did mention it. That is a lovely apartment, with a fabulous view. You stay as long as you need, Hollie."

Hollie smiled, thinking that she really should be feeling awkward now, staying in their apartment with no explanation. Instead, she had a calm feeling that no explanation was needed; if Samson wanted her to stay there, then his parents were fully accepting of the situation without any judgment or questions.

"Samson tells me you work part time at BB's Diner."

"Yes, I've been there for three years, since I started my veterinary degree."

His mum leaned forward. "I used to work in a restaurant as a waitress – best job I ever had. I absolutely loved it."

"I enjoy working at BB's, it's such a busy little restaurant and I love all the people I work with; they are like another family to me."

His mum wanted to hear more about the diner, the sort of food they served, the specials, how they made different dishes. It reminded her of her own youthful days as a waitress.

Samson took Hollie's plate. "I'll just put these into the kitchen, I'll be right back."

He didn't mind leaving Hollie with his mum – he trusted her not to say or do anything to make her feel awkward. Hollie didn't mind either.

"You must come over again, Hollie, when we don't have so many visitors. I'd like to hear more about the diner and I definitely would love to know all about the degree you're doing. It sounds so interesting."

Hollie smiled. There was a strange connection

between them. She felt that they had always been friends and this was just another quick chat at a family gathering.

"I'd like that."

Samson returned with another drink for Hollie and himself. His mum stood up.

"I should go and find Hector."

Samson sat close to Hollie, stretching his arm along the back of the settee. She moved towards him, leaning back on his arm, twisting her body round to face him.

"Your mother is so lovely. I can tell you are incredibly special to her."

He moved his head to glance into the next room where he could see his mother talking to some relatives.

"Yes, she is a special lady. She has always been there for me. Always putting me and Sophia first. I guess me and her have a special bond. We only had each other in those early years. She always told us that her love for Sophia and I got her through those bad days and kept her strong." He stretched his legs out in front.

"When it was only the three of us, I would help her with the shopping, the tea, and looking after Sophia while she went to work. When Hector came along, he took on that role, leaving me to go back to being a child again. For Mum, he gave her what she hadn't known before. Love."

Just by the tone of his voice, Hollie could tell that their mother-son relationship truly was a special one.

They both heard Sophia's voice in the next room become louder and closer. As she came into view, they could see a young man close behind her, being led by the hand.

"Hollie!" Sophia called out, eagerly making eye contact with Hollie. "I want you to meet Matt."

When they were almost in front of her and Samson, Matt stepped from behind Sophia. Samson stood up.

"Hello, mate," he said, holding out his hand to Matt. "Good to see you again. Come and sit with us."

Hollie smiled kindly at Matt – he seemed more anxious attending the family gathering than she was. Sophia and Matt sat down opposite them.

"This is Hollie; she's Samson's new girl."

Samson gave Sophia an intense stare as if to say *shut up*, but this had no effect on Sophia's ability to speak with no filter.

"He is besotted with her. I've never known him hang out with the same girl as much as this."

Hollie turned to look at Samson, worried that he

might be getting angry with Sophia, but he was obviously used to her straight talking. He just shrugged his shoulders, not looking embarrassed or bothered by her remarks at all.

"Come on, Matt, let's go get you a drink, mate – you look like you need it, hanging out with my sister."

The two men stood up and walked towards the kitchen. Matt's face began to change and Hollie could see him relax, laughing with Samson. Sophia got up and sat beside her and the two girls sat together chatting for a while. Sophia was certainly going to enjoy having a girl of a similar age in the family, almost like having an older sister. She was going to enjoy every moment of her new acquaintance. Every now and then, Hollie glanced over toward Samson – she could just about see him through the dining room leading into the kitchen. He knew she was looking at him as he looked back at her with his warm smile aimed right at her every time.

Hollie enjoyed talking to Sophia; she reminded her of Beth who was also rather excitable on most occasions. She could see Samson laughing with Matt and some other men in the kitchen.

After a short while, Samson returned.

"Come on Hollie, I'll take you home." He held out his hand to her. She stood up, catching hold of his hand, and turned to Sophia.

"It was lovely to see you again."

Sophia stood up and kissed her on each cheek.

"I'm so glad you came."

Samson led Hollie towards the garden where his mum and Hector were both talking to some friends. When they saw Samson and Hollie, they both walked across the patio towards them. Hector gave Hollie a kiss on the cheek.

"Thank you for coming, Hollie"

"Thank you for having me." She smiled at Hector. He had a charming elegance about him that she liked.

Hector gave Samson a brief hug.

"I'll ring you tomorrow; we must order those bathroom tiles."

"Yes, don't worry, I'll do that."

Samson's mother took Hollie's hand.

"It was a pleasure to meet you, Hollie. Please come round to see us again."

Samson leant over and gave his mum a hug, then kissed her on the cheek.

"I'll call you tomorrow."

He led Hollie out of the garden, down the driveway and towards the truck. It was dark now and the lanterns were shining brightly, dotted amongst the hedges down the driveway. Hollie let out a sigh of relief, pleased that she didn't embarrass herself and, above all, kept her white dress white.

Samson opened the truck door, helping her up the step. He drove back slowly, glancing over at her often. She was pleased that meeting the family was over, but she didn't want the evening with Samson to come to an end. She wondered if she might see him tomorrow.

He parked the truck on Stanley Street, opposite the apartment, then helped her down, placing his jacket around her shoulders.

"I'll walk you up."

She was pleased to have a bit longer with him.

"Thanks for today," she said, walking by his side. "For bringing Mrs Stuckey to see me, taking me to meet your family – I've had a really nice day."

Samson put the code into the keypad, releasing the lock on the front door. He held the door open for her.

"Let's take the lift, my feet are so tired."

Hollie pressed the call button for the lift. Seconds later, the doors opened and Hollie stepped in followed by Samson. She pressed the button for the third floor just as four men stepped into the lift. Samson nodded acknowledgement to them. Hollie felt uncomfortable and moved to the back of the lift.

One of the men began to stare at her, looking her up and down. Samson stepped in front of Hollie, blocking the man's view. The man looked away, pressing the lift to go up. The lift stopped at the next floor, the doors opened, and all four men got out. Samson waited till the doors closed then turned round to her.

"You okay?"

She stepped closer to him and he put his hand round her waist and pulled her closer. The lift door opened. He smiled at her and, taking her hand, they stepped out of the lift and walked up the hallway to the apartment door. Hollie swiped her card on the keypad then pushed the open the door.

Samson stood in the doorway.

"I'd better go," he said, then paused. "Thanks for coming to meet my family."

Hollie smiled, looking up at his eyes, then at his lips, hoping that he would kiss her before he left.

"Will I see you tomorrow?" she asked, moving fractionally closer.

Samson moved closer too.

"I want to see you every day." He placed both hands on her face then leaned forward and kissed her gently on her lips.

Passion bounced from one to the other, intensifying

the longer their lips were together. Hollie placed both her arms around his neck, gripping him tightly. Samson picked her up around her waist, pushing the front door shut with his foot. He carried her into the bedroom, his lips still on hers.

Hollie kicked off her pumps as Samson took his shirt off, unbuttoning his jeans and, pulling her close to his body, he undid the zip down the back of her white dress. It fell to the floor. He picked her up, laying her carefully on the bed. He kissed her body gently, starting from her stomach up to her chest, then her neck, then her lips. She didn't want him to stop. She had never known a man treat her with such attentiveness and caress her so gently. He brushed the hair away from her face.

"Are you sure you want to do this?" he asked softly.

She ran a hand over his broad shoulders, round his neck, then rested it on the side of his face.

"Yes, I do."

He reached into his jeans pocket, bringing out a condom packet. Hollie placed both her hands on either side of his face. His lips touched her face as she closed her eyes, feeling the passion between them increase. She had never experienced such intense sexual desire in a man while making love to her and she didn't want him to ever stop. He kissed her while holding her in his arms, wanting this moment with the girl he adored to last as long as it could. She was completely focused on just him. Nothing else mattered – only that moment between them which they were sharing. She wrapped her arms around him, not wanting to let go, holding her breath as she felt his hands run over her skin. Afterwards, he lay still for a moment, holding her tightly, still with his arms wrapped around her.

Hollie opened her eyes, looking straight into his. He kissed her, then she nestled her face under his.

"I don't want this night to end," Hollie said, looking up at him.

He smiled. "It doesn't have to end just yet. Why don't we go and sit on the balcony for a bit?"

Hollie quite liked the idea of that, sitting under the stars. Samson sat up before she could answer, slipping his legs into his jeans. He threw his shirt across the bed to her.

"Sounds like a lovely idea." She put her arms into his shirt, just doing up a couple of buttons. It had a strong smell of him which made her pull it closer to her. He smiled, seeing gaps of her skin between the undone buttons.

"Come on, I'll make us some coffee."

Hollie went out onto the balcony, into the night. The lights of the buildings and street lighting glimmered in front of her as far as she could see and, above her, the stars lit the sky. She leaned against the wall. Many windows were still lit up in houses, offices and apartments across the city. She imagined different people behind each window, living all quite different lives. None of which she would trade with the light behind her own window tonight.

Samson stepped out onto the balcony, passing her a mug of coffee, the smell alone awakening a smile.

"What are you looking at?"

"The city. It's so peaceful from up here. We can't see the chaos that's really going on down there."

He leaned with his back to the wall, facing her. She looked at him, dressed in just his jeans, his well-defined muscles running symmetrically down his chest and stomach and his matted hair clinging to the back of his neck.

"I'm meeting Beth and some of my university friends tomorrow evening. They're having a house party. Do you want to come with me?"

"Yeah, I'd love to come. I'd like to meet some of your student friends."

Hollie had taken Marcus to meet her university friends last year and it didn't go well. He took an instant dislike to them and was quite rude to them, then insisted that they left halfway through the evening. She'd felt so embarrassed that she told them she'd been feeling unwell to explain why she'd so left early.

"I can't promise that I'll fit in, though, but I'll try my best."

Hollie laughed; she didn't think he would ever behave as badly as Marcus.

"Don't worry, I know my friends will love you. Beth can't wait to see you again."

Samson had a roguish, rough look about him, but always acted like a true gentleman. What was not to love?

He took a mouthful of his coffee.

"Do you plan to house share while you do your last year at university?"

"I went to see the university accommodation office the other day and they have found me a flat share on campus."

He smiled. "You're all organised then. I thought you might have stayed here a bit longer. You know this place is empty for two more months."

She didn't want him to think that she was ungrateful because she was truly grateful for all that he had done for her; without him, she didn't know where she would be.

"Yes, I know, but I have to stand on my own two feet. I don't want to depend upon you or anyone else to find me somewhere to live. I earn my own money and I need to support myself through my last year."

He could see how important it was to her to be independent – after all, she had spent the last year being told what to do in almost every aspect of her life. He knew that he must let her lead and control her own life the way that she thought best.

"I understand. Just so you know, if you need me to help in any way, please ask."

She took a step closer to him and, reaching up, she kissed him softly on the cheek.

Someone above was certainly looking down on me kindly when they let me stumble on you, she thought.

He could see she was just starting to shiver from the cold night air.

"Come on, let's go back inside."

Hollie was pleased to get back into bed; it had been a long day and her eyes were now feeling heavy and ready to close. She kept Samson's shirt on as it felt comforting on her and she didn't want to sleep naked. He put the covers around her, lying close to her. Then he wrapped his arms around her, gently kissing her goodnight.

She closed her eyes with the feeling of being warm and happy and the thought that, at last, she had found someone who truly cared for her.

Chapter Nine

The morning sun was already high in the sky, the busy city rush over. A bin lorry slowly made its way up Stanley Street, stopping every few metres. Hollie woke to the sound of broken glass smashing into the bottom of the truck. She opened her eyes, but there was no arm around her, no warm body squashed against hers. She was in bed alone. She sat up, looking at the clock: it was mid-morning. She threw off the duvet, stepping onto the cold floor in bare feet.

Still wearing Samson's shirt, she opened the bedroom door and went into the hallway. She glanced towards the front door, looking for his shoes but they were gone. Still feeling hopeful, she walked into the kitchen, but he wasn't there: she was alone in the apartment. She made herself a coffee then sat on the settee. The sun was shining on the balcony and straight in through the glass doors into the lounge where she was sitting. As she slouched back, sipping her coffee, she caught sight of a folded piece of paper resting on the table in front of her. Her name was written across in bold. Thoughts began to race around her head of what Samson might have said in the note. She picked it up, turning it over to read his words.

"Hollie, sorry I left without saying goodbye. I needed to get an early start at the apartment. Will try to ring you later... Samson."

She folded the note up, placing it on the table with her coffee cup on top, then lay back on the settee. Not exactly what she was expecting, but then, what had she been expecting? To wake up in his arms again? She looked across the room to a beautiful painting of a couple standing in the rain, sharing a kiss under an umbrella. The picture held her dreamy romantic thoughts. She didn't know why he hadn't woken her to say goodbye. She couldn't help but think of his reputation, especially now that she had slept with him, if that was all it took for him to move on to the next. That empty, sad feeling swept through her body.

She took out her phone and rang Beth. After just a couple of rings, she heard her voice.

"Hello, hun, are you still at Samson's?" Hollie's mood lightened as soon as she heard her best friend's voice.

"Yes, I'm still here. I can't move into my university accommodation for another two weeks. I'm just ringing to check that we are still meeting at Jemima's this evening."

"Yes, definitely. Are you bringing Samson?"

Hollie could tell by the tone of her voice that she was already excited to see Samson again.

"I don't know if he can make it yet."

Beth quickly interrupted. "You better, girl. I can't believe you don't fancy him."

Hollie laughed.

"Beth, please, not everyone fancies one another just because they are the opposite sex. Apart from you, of course."

"I'll send you the address in case you don't have it. Shall we meet at the shop on the corner, then we can walk up the hill to Jemima's together?"

"Sure, I'll meet you at six."

"Alright, see you later."

Hollie ended the call, then quickly scrolled down to check if there had been any messages from Samson. There had been none. She took a deep breath, smelling in the scent of Samson from his shirt. The sunshine was now pushing through the glass doors and she could feel the warmth on her skin. She decided that she wouldn't mope around waiting for the clock to turn or for Samson to ring, but instead she'd get dressed and take a walk in that beautiful park across the road, tempted by what she seen from her bedroom window the previous day. She found a pair of jeans and a cropped shirt that tied into a knot at the front, perfect for such a walk.

Hollie didn't bother with any makeup, wrapping her hair up into a loose bun. She made her way out of the apartment, down the stairs, across the road and in through the grand iron gates that marked the entrance of the rather spectacular park. She stuck to the path as it twisted through the beautiful and well-maintained grassy lawn. Ahead she saw a humped bridge going over a small stream. Wildflowers covered the banks dropping down to the stream. She walked for about ten minutes, then a tall oak tree that stood alone caught her attention. She veered towards it across the grass. It didn't matter that she hadn't brought anything with her to sit on as the grass and the ground were both dry. She sat down, leaning forward, and hugged her knees, resting her chin on her arms.

The sun warmed her quickly and the intense brightness made her shut her eyes for a moment. She breathed out a sigh of contentment; at last she felt like she was leaving the past behind her. This was to be a new beginning, a new opportunity to enjoy her youth again. Something that she had pressed 'pause' on when she met Marcus a year ago. She had spent most of her first two years at university with Beth, but when she met Marcus, those special times and girly nights out slowed down to a halt.

Hollie's idea that Marcus was the right man for her was based on him being smart, well-groomed, confident and, most importantly, the fact that he had told her that he would always look after her. This was outweighed by his image of himself, his self-importance of what he thought he was, and taking control of all her decisions. Slowly, she had felt she was slipping into the person that Marcus wanted her to be, drowning, and becoming more out of reach for anyone to save her.

A couple were following the footpath, walking hand-in-hand, their dog beside them. They stopped to throw a ball, then the man kissed the woman, before taking hold of her hand again and continuing to walk through the park.

Hollie wondered why Samson hadn't been in a relationship. Maybe he wasn't looking for that. Did he really just sleep with a woman, then move on to the next? She guessed she would find out soon enough. She lay back, putting her hands behind her head. She still felt tired.

She woke to the sound of children playing with a ball close by. Sitting up with a start, she checked her watch; it was the middle of the afternoon. She glanced at her phone and could see Samson had sent her a message. Now smiling, she opened it.

"Hey, really busy with Hector, text me the address and I'll try to make it later ...Samson"

Great, she thought, *that sounds like the foundations for an excuse not to meet her later.* Her reply was simple:

"25 Archer Street, might see you later." She decided that no niceties were needed.

Hollie stood up, brushing the loose grass from her clothes, then made her way back to the apartment. She showered, then rummaged through her clothes to choose something that represented 'party girl'. She chose a red daisy-patterned skirt with a white cropped top.

Deep down, she knew that Samson wouldn't show tonight and therefore this was to be the first night of celebrating her single and independent life.

Leaving the apartment, she walked steadily to the bus-stop halfway down Stanley Street. Her shoes were high and narrow, not at all her usual footwear of comfy pumps. Her hair hung loosely over her shoulders, curls hanging down her back.

The bus stopped several times before it came to a halt on Archer Street. Hollie could see Beth standing outside the corner shop. She got off the bus with great care, not wanting to make a spectacle of herself by stumbling in her shoes.

"Wow, Hollie, you look amazing." The two girls wrapped their arms around each other with genuine affection.

"You look fabulous as usual, Beth."

Beth looked over Hollie's shoulder. "So, where is he, where is Samson?"

Hollie linked arms with Beth and the two girls started to walk up the hill towards Jemima's house, Hollie feeling much steadier on her feet while holding on to Beth.

"He's working," Hollie said. "I don't think he'll make it this evening."

Beth turned her head, looking at Hollie with wide eyes, raising her eyebrows.

"Don't look at me like that. We're not much more than friends. He has a different life to me. You forget, I'll be moving out soon, then we'll have no reason to see one another again."

Beth continued to look at Hollie in disbelief.

"No, Hollie, that's not what I saw the other day. The way he looks at you, the way you look back at him. Oh no, honey, he will be here tonight."

Hollie laughed at Beth's bold predictions.

"This must be it." Beth stopped, turning to face the green garden gate. "Number twenty-five. It's much bigger than I thought – how many housemates does she share with?"

Hollie took the lead, opening the gate and walking down the path towards the front door.

"I think she shares with six other students."

The Georgian house was spread over four floors. The girls walked into the grand entrance, the hallway stretching to the kitchen, the staircase winding its way up through the centre of the house. Loud music pumped from one of the downstairs rooms, vibrating through the floorboards under their feet. They went into the front room. Bay windows from wall to wall elegantly dominated the front. An extension on the back gave the house a huge amount of space. There were people everywhere: a group was spread out in the front room, some lying on the floor, some slouching over the settees. Jemima appeared from a crowd of guests.

"Hey, you two, I'm glad you both made it." She looked twice at Hollie. "You look so different – have you changed your hair or something?" She handed them both a glass of what appeared to be wine.

"No, same old me."

Hollie took the glass and took a huge gulp. She rarely drank anymore but from today she didn't have anyone else to think about or to apologise too.

"Cheers!" she said, clinking glasses with Beth who smiled and downed the entire contents. Hollie hesitated, then mirrored Beth, finishing her glass of wine.

Jemima led them both into another room at the back of the house.

"Peter and Freddy are both in here."

The room was full of people drinking and chatting. Hollie spotted their other two university friends, Peter and Freddy, on the other side of the room. Beth had sneakily picked up two more glasses of wine as Jemima led them through the kitchen and handed one to Hollie as Peter caught sight of them both. They made their way to the other side of the room; Jemima was distracted by some other guest and wandered off before they reached Peter and Freddy.

Peter gave both girls a kiss on the cheek, looking pleased to see them both.

"You both look amazing"

Peter and Freddy were both doing the same degree as Hollie and Beth. Peter was quite the charmer, while Freddy was shy, a little on the geeky side, but highly intelligent and the one that always came top of the class.

"You don't look too bad yourself," Beth said,

clutching hold of Peter's arm.

Hollie glanced at Beth, smirking unintentionally. Beth had fancied Peter since their first day of meeting at university. She had even joined the rowing club to spend more time with him, only he didn't seem to take the hint that she fancied him. Hollie had gone to support Beth during her first practice; her outfit was certainly not fit for purpose to suit the occasion: summer shorts and a low tight top showing off her cleavage wasn't appropriate for rowing, never mind that she struggled to row in time with her fellow teammates.

Hollie leaned over to kiss Freddy on the cheek, not wanting him to feel left out. Beth followed, not really wanting to take her hands off Peter. Beth downed her drink, looking at Hollie to follow.

"Shall I get you girls another drink?" Freddy asked, taking Beth's empty glass from her. Hollie finished hers and passed her empty glass to Freddy.

"Thanks, Freddy, I think I'll go with you." Hollie wasn't sure another drink was such a good idea and maybe if she went with Freddy, she would refill her glass with lemonade.

"I'll be back in a few minutes," Hollie said to her friend. Beth smiled, grateful to be left alone with Peter if only for a short while. Hollie followed Freddy to the kitchen, stepping over empty cans and bottles of beer.

The crates of beer were stacked up just inside the kitchen, with the empty ones leaning against the back door. Freddy helped himself to four bottles, handing two to Hollie. Two girls were sitting on a marble worktop, smoking, blowing their smoke through a small high window that was only slightly open.

"Hello, Freddy." He ignored them, embarrassed that they knew his name. He didn't need to acknowledge them; he knew exactly who they were. Last term, one of the girls had persuaded him to do their end of term assignment for them. Most girls were only interested in him for one thing: his knowledge. Except, of course, for Hollie; they had warmed to each other from day one. His nervous shyness and dedication to his veterinary degree at all times had been one of the reasons that she had wanted to make friends with him when they started.

"Just ignore them." Hollie looked daggers at the two girls, feeling pretty confident after a couple of drinks.

Freddy followed Hollie back to where they had left Beth and Peter. She could see that there were more people in the room now, and some had pushed the dining table against the wall and were sitting on top of it. It was getting a little smoky with what didn't smell like tabaco.

Beth pulled on Peter's arm.

"Shall we all go out into the garden?"

The other three liked that idea and followed Beth through the patio doors. The garden was busy too. A sound system belted out music at the top end and halfway down a small group of people surrounded a table, cheering and laughing loudly.

"Are they apple bobbing?" Freddy said, taking the lead to walk towards them.

"Hey, I used to love that party game as a child. I would always win the prize." Hollie said; she had many happy memories as a child at friends' birthday parties.

"I don't think that they're playing for sweets. It probably involves something a little more grown-up."

Hollie walked over as best she could, concentrating in her shoes on the uneven grass. The cheering got louder as they got closer. Two people were going head-to-head, dipping their heads into an old bathtub filled with cold water, with floating apples bobbing about. The boy closest to her was dunking his head in and out, grabbing an apple each time then releasing it into a bucket beside him. When he had ten apples in his bucket, he raised his left hand and was crowned the winner. His losing opponent was then handed a triple shot of something and, judging by the expression on the poor loser's face, it must have been an evil concoction.

The girl from the kitchen, who had taunted Freddy, took the place of the winner, waiting for a challenger to sit opposite her. Hollie knew she was good at this game and was desperate to see the look of defeat on the girl's face. Before Beth could stop her, she was already striding over, and quickly sat down on the stool facing her opponent.

Beth rushed to Hollie's side. "Are you sure about this?"

"Don't worry, I've got this," Hollie replied, feeling confident.

The lad running the game quickly went over the rules.

"Right girls, first one to take out ten apples using only their mouth, raise your left hand and you'll be declared the winner. Loser drinks from the cup of losers. Ready, steady, go."

Hollie ducked her head straight into the cold-water bath, biting into the first apple. The cold water shocked her into the reality of what the hell she was doing, but as she lifted her head out of the water and dropped her first apple into the bucket, she glanced over to see her opponent had already submerged her face in the water again, going for the second apple. Hollie's determination to win took over all other thoughts and feelings and she speeded up. Beth shouted continuously until Hollie had dropped the tenth apple into the bucket. Hollie raised her left hand, holding her breath while she looked across the bathtub. The girl still had her head submerged in the water. Hollie waited until she raised her head, then smiled, relieved that she had won.

"Well done," she said immediately to her losing opponent. She dried her face on a towel, got up and walked away with Beth.

"I can't believe you just did that," Beth said laughing, putting her arm round her.

Hollie laughed too. "Nor can I."

The two girls walked back up the garden to where Peter and Freddy were sitting. Hollie picked up her beer, drinking quickly from the bottle.

Jemima appeared from the house, carrying a bottle of fizzy wine. She walked towards them, placing it next to them with five glasses.

"Are you all having a good time?" She popped the cork out and poured the fizz into each glass.

"Cheers to us all. One more year at university together!"

They all clinked glasses with one another.

"Yes, here's to us." Beth knocked hers back.

Hollie took just one mouthful, thinking that this would be her last acholic drink of the night. She knew she would have to walk to the bus-stop with Beth later, then get the last bus home. Unless Peter took Beth home with him – then she would be going home on her own, so probably best not to have any more to drink.

The five friends chattered for some time in the garden, until it became dark and the only light was coming from the house. Peter finally put his arm around Beth, to which she responded by kissing him. Hollie, Jemima and Freddy turned their backs on them and continued to chat, mainly about study. Jemima stood up.

"I best get back into the house and check everyone is alright. I'll catch you guys later. On her way back in, she stopped to talk to someone, then pointed back down the garden towards them. She was blocking their view so Hollie couldn't see whom Jemima had stopped to talk to. She continued to talk to Freddy. Moments later, Hollie's eyes widened as the person walking down the garden towards them came closer for her to see.

Samson had spotted her. She forgot to breathe for a moment, then started to panic, thinking that he would be jealous or mad at her for sitting with Freddy. She looked at Beth, who was still kissing Peter. Hollie was sure that he would get the wrong impression and think that she was there with Freddy. Her heart was beginning to beat quickly and suddenly started to feel sick. Why was he here? She was sure he wouldn't show up.

Beth suddenly opened her eyes and at last stopped kissing Peter.

"Samson's here, I told you he would be, Hollie."

Samson reached the group, his eyes only on Hollie. His smile when seeing her lit up his face; he was so pleased to see her.

"Hey, I'm sorry I'm so late. I had to finish the bathroom with Hector. I hoped you wouldn't mind. I wanted to get it all done today so I could take tomorrow off and spend it with you."

Hollie breathed a sigh of relief; he wasn't cross at all, nor was he mad that she was sat rather close to another man. Samson took his eyes off her for a moment, sitting down on the grass next to Freddy.

"Hello, mate, I'm Samson. You must be one of Hollie's university friends." He held out his hand to Freddy. Freddy shook it, relieved too that he was such a nice bloke.

"Hello, Beth, you're looking stunning, a pleasure to see you again."

Beth was pleased that Samson had shown up.

"We were waiting for you, weren't we Hollie?"

Hollie wasn't feeling too well. "I think I might be sick."

She stood up, giddiness taking hold, and tried to walk further down the garden. Her legs were not working properly in line with her body and she fell to her knees, vomiting up the liquid that was in her stomach. Samson jumped to his feet, rushing over to her. He knelt down beside her, holding her hair back with one hand and placing his other hand around her, trying to steady her, not wanting her to fall forward onto the ground. Her head was spinning, her throat was sore and she felt like a complete idiot. Beth sat on the other side of her, handing a tissue that she had just found in her bag.

Samson turned to Beth. "I think I'll take her home. Do you need me to drive you home too, Beth?" He took off his jacket, putting it around Hollie, then helped her to her feet, allowing her to lean on him and taking her full weight.

"Thanks, Samson, you are a gem, but Peter said he will see me home. I think you have your hands full with getting Hollie home."

"Goodbye, Beth, nice to meet you, Peter and Freddy."

Hollie was now standing upright; she turned slightly to look at Samson.

"I think I'll manage to walk on my own, thank you." Her stubbornness was digging in for now. She let go of Samson completely, and took off her shoes.

185

Carefully, she placed one foot in front of the other, concentrating on staying upright.

"I don't need you to come and rescue me tonight."

Samson took a step back away from her, not wanting her to think that he was only there to rescue her from this situation.

Hollie drifted from right to left till she eventually reached the house. Samson followed, trying not to walk too close, but not too far if she were to fall. He stepped closer as she negotiated the steps.

"I didn't think you would show up tonight," she said, holding the straps of her shoes with one hand, gripping the garden wall with the other.

Samson looked at her, confused with her comment. "Why would you think that?"

"Because you left this morning without waking me, leaving me a 'might see you later' note."

He opened the garden gate for her, offering his arm for her to hold.

"But I didn't want to wake you. You looked so peaceful. I thought you needed the sleep."

Hollie refused to take his arm, continuing to stumble, now walking in bare feet on the pavement.

"You should have woken me to say goodbye. I woke up alone."

Samson opened the truck door for her, not wanting to offer to help only to be refused again. He stood back as he didn't want her to think that he thought she was incapable of getting herself in. She lifted her leg up as high as she could, placing her foot on the step, but she couldn't pull herself up. Her head was dizzy and nothing was in focus.

Samson couldn't watch her struggle so he moved closer, placing his hands around her waist and lifting her up onto the seat.

"Thank you, but I would have managed."

Samson got in and started to drive.

"I'm sorry, I'm really not very good at relationships. I don't seem to know what the right thing to say or do to make you happy."

Hollie looked towards him, still not able to focus on him properly.

"Did you say relationship? As in girlfriend, boyfriend?" Hollie couldn't help but start laughing. Had she not consumed as much alcohol as she had, she would have found such a remark quite sweet but at that moment she found it hilarious. All day she had convinced herself that he wasn't the relationship kind of guy, and now this. She placed her hand over her mouth to try to silence her laugh.

Samson glanced over to her.

"You are my girl, aren't you? I haven't really had a girl before, not that you belong to me, but what I meant to say is, you're the only girl for me."

Hollie suddenly stopped being cross and looked at him, her heart beating quickly.

"I think I'm going to be sick again."

He quickly pulled over, parked on a grass verge, then jumped out. Hollie had already stumbled out of the truck and was kneeling vomiting onto the grass.

"I can't remember the last time I felt this awful. I don't know what I was thinking, drinking so much. I barely drink anything at all usually."

She staggered to her feet, too tired and unwell to walk. Samson picked her up, lifting her carefully back into the truck, tucking his jacket around her. He continued the drive back to the apartment. Hollie rested her head on the side of the seat, trying to keep as still as possible. She closed her eyes in the hope that the world would stop spinning, but it didn't.

Samson drove in silence, not wanting to disturb her, and she didn't want to talk as it would only add to the vibrations already in her head. Once they were parked on Stanley Street, Hollie opened the door and stepped out, placing her bare feet on the pavement. Samson locked up the truck.

"Shall I carry you?"

"Thank you, but I'll walk." She picked up her shoes and started walking slowly towards the door which Samson opened for her.

"Shall we take the lift?"

"I don't think my stomach could take it," she said, placing her hand on her tummy. "I think I'll walk up the stairs."

She held on to the bannister, lifting one foot at a time on to the next step, Samson following a few steps behind. Suddenly, she stood still; her head was spinning and all she wanted was to lie down, desperately soon. She turned around to him, her eyes red, her face pale. He moved up to the step below her. She leaned forward and, reaching out, she put her arms round his neck. He lifted her up into his arms, carrying her up to her floor. Samson opened the apartment door and went into the bedroom, laying her carefully on her side on the bed. Her eyes remained closed. He pulled the duvet over her, leaving her fully clothed. He could remember seeing a bucket in the cleaning cupboard which he fetched and put next to the bed. As he had done before, he dragged the mattress from the spare bedroom, placing it next to her bed. Knowing that she would need it when she woke, he placed a glass of water next to her bed. Then he sat beside her for a few minutes, watching her sleep. *Why had she laughed when he suggested that she was his girlfriend? Why was that so ridiculous to her?*

Chapter Ten

The morning sun pushed its way through the slits in the blinds, bringing sunlight into the room. Hollie wasn't yet ready to greet the day. Noise from the traffic on the street outside meant she couldn't get back to sleep. Reluctantly, she opened her eyes. She lifter her pounding head off the pillow, hoping that a more upright position would reduce the thumping. The sight of a glass of water was a pleasant welcome to the day and she drank it in one go. Looking down, she could see a bucket on the floor, prompting her memory of the night before. Immediately, she turned over, laying her head back on the pillow. She could now see Samson sitting on the mattress which lay parallel to her bed on the floor. He was awake, drinking coffee.

He smiled. "How are you feeling? Do you want some coffee?"

She sat up, brushing her hair back from her face,

knowing she must look a mess.

"I'm so sorry for last night. I feel so ashamed – that wasn't really me. I don't know why I drank so much. Please don't take any notice of anything I did or said," she said, desperately trying to recall the evening. "I hope I didn't say anything to offend you, did I?" She could remember being sick.

"You are quite adorable when you're drunk. I'll get you some coffee."

Hollie realised that she was still dressed in the clothes from last night. Samson returned came back with coffee, placing her mug on the table beside her bed.

"Can I get you anything else?"

"No, thank you," she said, taking a sip from the mug, assuring herself that the coffee would kick-start her back into life.

"I don't know why you look after me so well. I must be such a burden to you. You are constantly having to come and fetch me from some sort of situation that I've got myself into. I really don't know why you bother." She placed the mug on the table, then twisted her hair to one side, letting it hang down her shoulder. "I've seen the way other girls look at you – why don't you choose one of them? One that is less of a bother to you."

She felt foolish for the way that she had acted last night. Somehow, she had misread Samson's intentions, causing her to act like a spoilt child.

"Please don't say that; you're nothing like other girls. Things that matter to you and things that you care about are not important to most girls. I know that you always see the good in people. You are the kindest person I have ever known. The day I met you in the hallway, outside my apartment, I felt something I have never felt before. I knew…" He paused for a moment, smiling gently. "I knew that I wanted to get to know you better."

Hollie knew that any man who could say such nice words to her while looking at her dressed in clothes from the night before, make-up smudged round her eyes and sick in her hair, was certainly worth a chance. She smiled at him.

"I really thought when you weren't here when I woke yesterday, that I wouldn't see you again. I'm sorry, I was wrong."

Samson moved closer to her, putting his hand on her face.

"I know you think I have a reputation for being with a girl once, then moving on, but it feels different with you. Please give me a chance."

He leaned closer still to her and kissed her on the lips. She felt every nerve in her body tremble. She lifted her hand, running it over the stubble on his face. Their eyes remained locked on each another as Samson moved back. Hollie felt grubby and messy.

"I think I should have a shower."

He gave her a cheeky smile and pulled her close to him once again but she softly pushed him back.

"A shower on my own." She smiled at him, throwing back the duvet, making her way to the bathroom. She closed the door slightly, knowing he wasn't the type of man to just walk in after her without being invited.

After a hot shower, Hollie felt so much better. She found herself a clean pair of jeans and a blue and white checked blouse. Slipping on her canvas shoes, she went to find Samson. He was lying with his hands behind his head across the settee, watching sport on the television. The moment she walked into the room, he turned his head and sat up, his attention now on her.

"Where do you want to go today?" she asked as she sat down next to him, her hair still wet and held back with a clip. He looked at her pretty face, just wanting to kiss her again.

"I thought we could go to the seaside — what do you think?"

Hollie's face immediately lit up with excitement.

"Really? I'd love to go to the seaside!" Her thoughts

were of home. "My parents live near the sea in Cornwall. I love looking out to sea, being on the beach, watching the rough sea crash over the rocks. It must be one of my favourite places."

Samson was relieved that she liked the idea of a trip to the coast. He himself had fond memories of trips to the seaside with his mum, Sophia and Hector on special occasions. Even now, as an adult, it still felt like a special treat if he had the opportunity to go, and today was a special day.

"I haven't done a picnic, though. I thought we might just have fish and chips."

Hollie put her hand on her stomach.

"Sorry, perhaps I shouldn't have mentioned food," he said as he stood up and grabbed his keys from the table. "Come on, let's go."

Hollie grabbed her cardigan on the way out, following him down the stairs and outside. The sun was shining and a light breeze blew, keeping the warm morning a little cooler. Busy people rushed towards them with shopping bags, some dressed for work carrying briefcases or satchels. Catching hold of Samson's hand in the busy street, Hollie took no notice. He gripped it back tightly, as though he was never going to let go. The truck was just a short walk away and as he opened the door for her, he kissed her on the cheek before releasing her hand, wanting to reassure her that he had no intention of running off and that yesterday he hadn't meant to upset her by leaving her alone.

He started the engine and pulled out of Stanley Street. Hollie stretched out her legs, looking across at him. Marcus had never taken her anywhere special, even in those early months, not just the two of them. Samson really did seem to want to make her happy. This was certainly a new feeling for her; accepting it could be more difficult than she thought. His affection and desire to look after her were quite overwhelming, something she hadn't experienced from anyone before.

"Have you heard anything from Marcus?" Samson asked, glancing quickly at her.

"No, surprisingly and thankfully – nothing," she replied. "I didn't think he would walk away so easily."

"That's good, he must have got the message."

Hollie was expecting him to say something like, "How did you get involved with someone like him?" but he didn't say anything.

They drove for over an hour. Hollie was still feeling tired from the previous night. Watching the countryside go past was comforting. Sheep and cattle grazing in fields had once been a familiar sight, a sight that she knew she had taken for granted. She didn't realize how much she had missed it until now.

"I'm planning to visit my family down in Cornwall before I start back at university."

Samson took his eyes off the road for a moment, looking at her as if to say he didn't want her to go anywhere away from him.

"I'm sure you must miss them. It must be difficult being so far away from them."

Hollie pictured them sat around the kitchen table having lunch together.

"Yes, I do, but it is a life that I chose to leave behind, to find a better one. If I had stayed, I would be working in the local shop or post office. The village where I grew up is beautiful and my parents' farmhouse is on the edge of a village, looking down to the harbour. Maybe one day I'll return to live there."

She thought for a moment about what her parents would think of Samson. Her mother would be worried for her, jumping into another relationship too quickly. Marcus had certainly charmed her into thinking that he was the right man for her daughter. After all, she only wanted her to be happy and she had convinced herself that Marcus would soon become her son-in-law. Little could she have seen past the exterior of who he really was.

"Maybe you could come with me if you can get the time away from work. I'd like to show you around my village."

Samson turned his head, eyes wide in disbelief at the unexpected invitation.

"I'd like that." He was playing down his excitement at her treating him as her boyfriend. "I've only got another three days to finish the renovations, then just some painting that I could do in an afternoon. Hector has already found someone to rent the apartment. They want to move in at the end of the month, so I need to get it finished in two weeks."

"Where will you live then?" Hollie asked, concerned that his next project would be further away.

"I'm not too sure yet. Hector has just purchased an apartment at auction. It's just a few blocks up from Stanley Street but it needs a complete renovation. It's barely habitable so I'll probably move back home with my parents for a while."

Hollie smiled, relieved that he wouldn't be too far away from her.

"My university accommodation is only a few minutes' drive from your mum's house, so easy enough for you to come over."

She had no idea where this relationship was going, and it was probably moving too quickly, but despite this, she knew that being with him made her happy.

"It feels like we've known one another for a long

time," Hollie said, looking at him while he drove.

Samson smiled, taking in a deep breath; he had no idea how to put his feelings about her into words. At last, he had found someone that he connected to, but was scared that he would do something to lose her.

"Yeah." He was playing it cool. "It certainly doesn't seem like I first saw you just over a week ago."

He turned off the main road, driving down a narrow lane that ended at a junction. He indicated left, driving along the promenade beside the sea. Cars were parked at an angle on one side. He parked in the first empty space he saw.

Hollie breathed in the familiar sea air that she loved. Closing her eyes for a moment, a peaceful feeling swept through her. She got out of the truck and leaned against the wall. The tide was out and, in the distance, she could see small white waves creeping up the beach. There was a wide path that ran parallel between the beach and the road. Samson caught hold of her hand as they started to walk. Her head was still a little fuzzy so she was pleased to be out in the fresh air. In the distance, she saw some shops and the bright lights of an amusement arcade. As they got closer, the area became busier and a large group of people were hanging out outside the amusement arcade. The children's rides were lit up with colourful, flashing lights, loud music adding to the thrilling atmosphere. Samson gently pulled Hollie's hand as they crossed the road. On the other side, someone called to them from the group congregated outside the amusements.

"Samson!"

Samson took a moment to focus on the man who was calling him.

"Hey, Toff!" he shouted back once he had recognised him. He turned to Hollie. "Do you mind if we go over and say hello? He's an old college friend of mine."

"Sure," she replied, quite keen to meet any of his friends. Crossing the road, Samson shook hands with Toff.

"It's good to see you mate! It's been a while. How are you?"

Toff had blond, mousey hair, and was dressed in long shorts and a vest top. He looked pleased to see Samson.

"Good to see you too, mate. It must be three or four years. Last time I saw you, you'd just started a new job at that electrical company." Remembering his manners, he looked at Hollie. "And who's this pretty lady?"

"This is Hollie." Samson put his arm around her

waist, moving closer to her. Hollie smiled at Toff.

"I hope you've settled him down, Hollie. Samson was quite the rogue at college."

Samson laughed. "I think you led me into that reputation, mate. What are you doing here? Are you on a day trip?"

"I wish I were, Samson. My girlfriend got pregnant last year and then I lost my job as an electrician, so we had to move in with her mother who lives here. It was only supposed to be temporary but I can't get any work here and it's too expensive for me to travel back and forth to the city."

"Sorry to hear that. Surely you can get a job that will pay enough to make it worth the commute?"

"I'm always looking. We don't have a car so relying on public transport is difficult."

A young woman pushing a pram walked up to them; she stopped next to Toff, who placed his arm around her.

"This is Jodie, my girlfriend, and little Rosie in the pram."

Samson shook Jodie's hand.

"This is my old college mate, Samson, and his girlfriend, Hollie."

"Hello, Hollie." Jodie shook hands with Hollie. "Are you here for a day trip?"

Hollie smiled. "Yes, Samson drove us down for a day out. You must love living so close to the sea. You're very lucky."

Jodie's face didn't give Hollie the impression that she felt lucky at all.

"To be honest, Hollie, I wish we lived in the city. Toff can't get work here and we couldn't possibly move back to the city because the rent would be too expensive for us to manage on Toff's wage alone. So, for now we are stuck here living with my mother." She looked at Toff, who retuned her look with a smile. "But we're alright," he said. "Something will turn up."

Samson crouched down to get a closer look at Rosie in the pram.

"And you've got this ray of sunshine," he said as he smoothed the side of her face. Rosie wiggled her arms, making cooey sounds in delight at Samson's attention.

"Oh, she likes you, Samson," Jodie said.

He stood up, still smiling down at Rosie.

"She's gorgeous." He looked at Toff. "Give me your phone number and I'll keep a look out for some work in the city. I'll give you a ring if I find something that might suit you."

"Cheers, mate, that's great. I really appreciate that."

Toff found a packet in his pocket and scribbled down a phone number, then passed it to Samson.

"It was good to see you, Toff. Good luck with everything."

"You too, mate." He put his arm round Samson's shoulder. "You two take care. It was a pleasure to meet you, Hollie. Maybe we'll see you again."

Hollie smiled. "Yes, I hope so."

Jodie smiled at Hollie. "Maybe we'll come visit you in the city if ever we move ever move back."

"That would be nice." There was a warm friendliness about the couple that made her hope that one day they would have some good luck, and Toff would find the job he needed to support them.

As Samson and Hollie walked hand-in-hand along the pavement that ran beside the beach, Samson talked about his old friend.

"I can't believe that Toff has ended up unemployed. He was such a good electrician at college, always coming top of the class. We all thought that he was destined to do better than any of us, possibly having his own electrician business. It's strange how things often take a different path."

"Do you think you can find him a job as an electrician?"

"Yeah, that's the easy bit. It's finding a place to

rent that they can afford on one wage – that's the difficult bit."

"Rosie was a sweetie, wasn't she? I think she liked you."

Samson smiled. "Yeah, she was gorgeous. Do you imagine you'll have children one day?"

She looked at him. "I suppose my biggest dream was to do my veterinary degree, then, in order: career, marriage, children. Maybe a little old-fashioned. I do know that I would like a big family. Family is so important to me and I look forward to having my own one day. What about you? You don't strike me as the marrying, settling down type."

Samson laughed. "Is that really the impression that I give you? I would like to marry one day, but it's not a priority for me. Having children is a big commitment that I would take seriously. My early childhood wasn't great, so I know first-hand the importance of having good parents. When Hector showed up in my life, he showed me what a father's role in a child's life really was. If I could be as good a father as Hector was to me, then I'll be a good dad."

They walked past the fish and chip shop. Samson took in a deep breath, clearly enjoying what he could smell.

"That smells good! Shall we get some lunch and sit on the beach?"

"Mmmm. I still feel a little delicate, but maybe I could manage a small portion of fish and chips."

They walked down some steps that led them on to the beach. Hollie removed her pumps, enjoying the feeling of warm sand on the soles of her feet. They found a quiet spot just below the sand dunes, and sat down on the soft sand. Hollie unwrapped her parcel and took a small bite.

"What's your plan when you finish your degree?"

"Right now, I'll concentrate on my final year, then next summer I'll start applying for jobs – maybe some local veterinaries to start with, but really I'd prefer to work with farm animals. I'm keen on animal welfare and I'd prefer to live in the country; however, farm vet jobs are few and far between. I guess I'll have to take whatever I'm offered to start with." She took another small bite, enjoying the taste but worried how her stomach will react. "How about you, Samson? Will you always be a city boy?"

"I guess so. I've never really lived anywhere else. I've always lived close to Sophia, Mum and Hector. I'm not sure I'd like too much distance between us."

Hollie looked out to sea. "There's something quite magical about the ocean. The whole world is out there, waiting to be explored. Not by me, on my waitress's wage, though."

She lay back on the warm sand, resting her head

on Samson's hoodie that he had thrown on the sand.

"You've done well, though. You and Hector have built quite an empire of rental accommodation. Will Hector hand it all over to you one day to manage?"

"Maybe. I like working with him, he teaches me things that I need to know, not about electrics or plumbing, but more about people skills and good business skills." He leaned back on the sand, placing his elbow next to Hollie, then resting his head on his hand. As he brushed her hair back from her face, a shudder went down her body and she closed her eyes for a moment.

The sun was high in the clear blue sky. A breeze blew off the sea and up the beach towards them, cooling the. Samson looked down at Hollie; her wounds, still visible from the previous week, were healing. She opened her eyes to see him looking directly at her. He smiled and she felt warm and comfortable having him so close to her. The warm sun made her feel sleepy. They lay together for a while, listening to the waves rolling over each other as they crept up the sand.

After almost an hour Hollie, opened her eyes and sat up.

"Did I fall asleep?" she asked, looking at Samson who was lying back on the sand. He was wide awake and clearly hadn't fallen asleep.

He laughed. "Yeah, you did, but don't worry, you didn't snore too loudly."

Hollie pushed him; he retaliated by grabbing her waist and lifting her over him, lying her back on the sand again. His face was close to hers now. She placed her hand softly on his face. Kissing her on the lips, he moved his body closer. She placed her other hand on his face, not wanting him to stop kissing her. After a few moments, he stopped and looked at her.

"I could kiss you all day."

She smiled at the thought of that.

"Come on, let's walk back," he said, and stood up, pulling her to her feet. Hollie picked up his hoodie and her pumps, then caught hold of his hand as they began to walk back along the sand towards the road. She felt relaxed with him, she didn't feel as though she had to please him or behave in a certain way for him. It was so nice to be herself, and that alone was what he liked about her. This was the happiest she had been in a long time. She thought that she would ring her mum that evening and tell her all about him, then possibly plan a visit back home, taking him with her.

They walked back passed the chip shop and a row of gift shops, then crossed onto the opposite side of the road from the beach, walking up a side street with houses on either side.

"What are those men doing?" Hollie stopped, pointing up an alleyway to a group of young men standing close together.

"I'm not sure, but it looks like they're causing trouble. Come on, let's walk on." Samson looked away and continued walking but Hollie was still fixed on the group of men.

"Is that a man on the ground?"

Samson stopped, looking up the alleyway; there were garages on one side and a high brick wall on the other. He could see a man, lying on the floor, who was being repeatedly kicked by one of the other men.

"Oh no, that's awful, what shall we do?"

"Let's walk on and ring the police," he said, taking out his phone.

Hollie took one last look, trying to get a good description of any of the men to give to the police.

"Oh no! I think it's your friend Toff who's being kicked!"

Samson immediately stopped and looked down the alleyway where he could see Toff's distinctive toffee-coloured curly hair.

"I've got to go and help him." He looked around. "Go and wait in that shop over there," he said, pointing to a newsagent across the street. "Please don't come with me."

She nodded as he ran in the direction of the men who heard him heading towards them. The man stopped kicking Toff, who was now curled up on the ground, trying to shield himself from the brutal attack. Samson thumped the attacker who fell back, then another man stepped forward, ready to strike, but Samson was too quick – with no hesitation, he launched his fist at him, sending him to the ground. There were six more men, all of whom looked pretty angry, but Samson was confident and showed no signs of being intimidated by so many.

"Go home, all of you, unless you want me to knock you all down one by one."

One of the men decided to chance himself against Samson and lunged towards him. Samson took him down with a single punch. Toff, realising his attacker had stopped, lifted his head. Seeing Samson, he tried to get up, but fell back down, clutching his ribs.

"Stay there, mate. I'll just get rid of these jokers then ring you an ambulance."

He turned to face the remaining men, ready for the next opponent. Suddenly, from the corner of his eye, he caught sight of two figures coming towards him. He froze when he saw that one was Hollie, who was followed by a young man holding her close with a knife against on her neck.

"Does this belong to you?"

Samson looked straight at Hollie; he could see how frightened she was.

"On your knees, tough guy."

Samson dropped to his knees.

"Hurt her and I'll kill you!"

He focused on the man holding Hollie; anger was flowing through him like a ravine. Every vein in his body was pumping with fury and he had to restrain himself from launching an attack on the man, worried that the risk of Hollie being hurt before he got to him were too high. One of the other men stepped forward, stood in front of him and took a swing at his face with his clenched fist; he lost focus for a moment then stared at the man still holding Hollie. The man took another swing at him, this time drawing blood from his face. Tears began to fall down Hollie's face; she couldn't bear to watch him be punched again and again. She reached behind her, grabbing what she could between her attacker's legs in one hand, squeezing as hard as she could with every bit of strength she had. Immediately, he released the grip he had on her, enabling her to break free from his grasp. Samson was already on his feet, taking a swing at the man who had hit him, his fist making contact with his face, blood splattering from the man's nose as he fell to the ground. Next, Samson quickly turned to the man who had held Hollie, kicking the knife from his hand, then taking a swing at him which sent him flying to the ground. The other two men started to run back up the alleyway.

Samson turned around to look at Hollie.

"Are you hurt?" She ran to him and he wrapped his arms tightly around her.

"I'm sorry, I should have gone to the shop and waited like you said but instead I rang the police then came a bit further down the alley to see if you were alright." She still had tears running down her face and was trying to catch her breath.

He held her tightly. "It's okay now, we're okay."

Still on the ground, Toff tried to struggle to his knees. "Thanks mate. I'm so sorry."

Samson tried to help him to his feet, but he couldn't get up.

"Don't get up. Who were those guys? Did you know them?"

Toff couldn't look at Samson; he lay back down on the ground. "Yeah, I owe them money and they wanted it back."

"Toff, what have you got yourself into?"

They could hear the ambulance and police sirens coming closer. Samson had blood running down his face. Hollie dabbed it with the sleeve of her cardigan. The ambulance parked close by, the paramedics going first to assess Toff. Minutes later, they lifted him onto a stretcher and took him into the ambulance. Samson went over to him when they had made him comfortable.

"You'll be alright, mate; I'll give you a ring in a few days."

Toff held out his hand to catch hold of Samson's. "I'm really sorry for all this."

Samson smiled, stepping away to let the paramedics close the doors. The police took statements from him and Hollie.

"Are you sure that you don't want the paramedics to look at that wound?" the policeman asked Samson, putting the statements away in a folder.

"No thanks, it's really only a scratch." He took hold of Hollie's hand. "Come on, let's go home."

Hollie was relieved to get back in the truck and head home. Samson sighed deeply as he pulled out onto the road. The journey back home was mostly silent, until they got much closer to the city.

"I'm really sorry for today," Samson said, looking at Hollie. She didn't respond, she just stared out of the window. "I just wanted to spend the day together, just you and me." She was still in shock from what had just happened and really didn't want to talk. She had felt afraid before, many times when Marcus had threatened her or made her think he would crash the car during an argument, or even when he had hit her; she'd felt frightened but didn't care enough about herself to be scared about whether she lived or died. Today was different – she did care about her life and she cared very much for Samson's, too.

She looked over at him; his face had stopped bleeding but had now swollen up just below his eye. He looked back at her, seeing his blood on her cardigan, her face still scared.

"Maybe you shouldn't be with me. I always seem to find trouble. You should be with someone who stays away from violence, someone who can take care of you better." He concentrated on the road ahead, thinking that today he had probably pushed her away, making her think twice about going out with a guy who walks into bother, throwing punches all the time. Maybe he wasn't the right man for her. Her silence assured him that his feelings and thoughts were right.

In Stanley Street, he parked a short distance from the apartment block and switched off the engine, resting both hands on top of the steering wheel. Hollie released her seatbelt then turned to face him.

"No-one has ever protected me and shown that they truly care about me more than you. Right now, I don't want to be with anyone else but you."

He looked up, surprised that she wasn't giving him

the 'sorry but it's not going to work' speech. She fixed her eyes on him, waiting for his reply.

Gritting his teeth together, trying not to show the emotions that he was struggling to hold in, he said, "Hollie, I care about you very much. I've never wanted to be with anyone the way I want to be with you."

She smiled, bringing the sunshine back into her face. Leaning over, she kissed him.

"Come on, let's go home."

Samson was out of the truck in a flash, putting his arm around her as they walked up to the apartment. He felt happy that she still wanted him and held her close. Inside the apartment, Hollie went into the kitchen to find some warm water, a cotton dressing and some ice.

"Go and sit down and I'll clean up your face."

Samson sat down on the settee. "It's fine, really. Please don't fuss."

She returned with a bowl of warm water in which she dipped the cotton dressing before gently cleaning the blood from his face. With a clean dressing, she wiped the wound dry. Samson couldn't take his eyes off her as she carefully tended to his face. She stopped, then looked at him, her face close to his. He pulled her closer. She lost her balance and fell onto his lap.

"Hey, I haven't finished yet," she said, smoothing his face with her hand. He put his arms around her and stood up, lifting her with him and heading towards the bedroom with her in his arms. As they entered the bedroom, he carefully put her feet on the ground, her arms still clinging around his neck. His arms tightened around her waist, kissing her lips, pulling her towards him.

Hollie felt her heart pounding. She wanted him now. She backed up, falling onto the bed. He flung his T-shirt on the floor as she started unbuttoning her blouse. He knelt on the bed, unzipped her jeans, then gave a gentle tug till they fell on the floor. He paused for a moment, looking at her almost naked body. He kissed her stomach, continuing up to her breasts, then her lips. Hollie held her breath while he reached down to take a condom from his jeans pocket. She knew that, at last, she had found someone that she could truly love with every bit of her body. Sex wasn't a chore with Samson, but a feeling of passion, extreme sexual tension coursing between them. He was so gentle, touching every part of her body. She held on to him, not wanting to ever let go.

Afterwards, he pulled her naked body against his until she could feel his heart beating next to hers, then pulled the duvet over them, lying behind her while she lay her head on his arm, tucked under his chin, pushed against his chest with his arms securely around her. After a few moments, she heard a change in his breathing, indicating that he had probably fallen asleep. Hollie smiled and closed her eyes, knowing that she was falling in love with him.

Chapter Eleven

The morning came too soon for Hollie. Her eyes were wide open but her body was tired and unresponsive. She faced the window and watched the daylight flood into the room. Samson lay close behind her, his arm draped round her waist, his hand tucked under her tummy. She smiled, feeling like a small animal in hibernation, not needing to move from this moment for weeks. Samson woke up and turned onto his back, stretching his arms above the pillow until his hands hit the wall. Hollie rolled over and put her head on the pillow beside him. He turned his head to face her.

"Hey," he said, pushing her hair of her face. "Did you sleep alright?"

"I think I did; I've no idea why I feel so tired. I feel as though I could sleep for days."

"Why don't you stay in bed a while? I've really got

to get up and do some work."

She touched the side of his face, outlining the small lump just above his eye and the cut which still looked sore.

"I've promised to meet up with Beth today – she needs to buy a dress for a family wedding and she's asked me if I'll help her choose. I've no idea why she needs my opinion as she has a dress sense all of her own."

"Well, I've got to call into the building merchants to pick up some pipes. Hector wants to show me the apartment that he's purchased this afternoon but I should be back by 6 o'clock. Let me cook you some tea."

She smiled at such a sweet gesture. "That's kind of you but I should cook for you since you're the one who's working all day."

"No, please," he interrupted. "Let me. Let me show you I can be domesticated and can cook."

He decided that as soon as he left the apartment, he would ring his mum and ask her to suggest the simplest, but most impressive, meal possible. He kissed Hollie on the cheek, happy and content to have woken up beside her.

"Oh, I nearly forgot, Sophia wants to come round later to see you."

He pulled back the covers, stood up, then headed straight for the shower. Hollie remembered she was naked, so once she heard the shower water running, she darted across the room to find a T-shirt to slip over her head before diving back under the duvet. Samson returned after a few minutes, picked up his own T-shirt off the floor where he'd thrown it last night. Hollie sat up in bed.

"Maybe you should bring some clothes back with you if you're going to be staying here with me?"

He looked up from buttoning his jeans, smiling at her suggestion.

"I will."

He stepped towards her, leaning over the bed and placing both hands on either side of her face then kissed her gently on her lips. Was this what it felt like to be in a relationship, behaving like a couple? He liked this new feeling.

"So, I'll see you tonight?"

She caught hold of his hand as he pulled away, giving a gentle tug. Needing little persuasion, he returned to kiss her again.

"Remember, ring me if you need me." He walked towards the door, looking back with a smile.

"Go to work, I'll see you later."

Hollie lay back on the pillow for a moment. She

turned to her side, reaching for her phone to text Beth the plans for meeting later. |She forced herself to throw off the covers and headed straight into the shower, hoping that would wake her up for the day. Beth was never going to believe the day she'd experienced yesterday!

She was soon heading out the door, biting into a croissant that had been left in the fridge a couple of days previous. As planned, Beth was waiting in the doorway of their favourite coffee shop. As soon as she saw Hollie, she quickly walked over to greet her with a friendly hug and kiss on the check. They were so pleased to see one another.

"I can't wait to hear everything about Peter," Hollie said, smirking.

Beth caught hold of her arm, leading the way into the coffee shop, where they soon found a table and ordered coffee.

"Well?" Hollie said, waiting for Beth to start. She could tell from her face that she was bursting with news to tell her.

"Peter is such a gentleman! He walked me home and we had a passionate kiss in the porch. My mum, being nosy, came to the door, putting any further action on hold. Well, after I introduced him, she invited him in for a bit. That was alright but then she asked him to come round for dinner the following evening. What a nightmare! I've been waiting years to date this guy and the first date is tea with my mum and dad. All I needed was for Uncle Jessy and Aunty Mabel to get an invite and it truly would have been finished before we even got started."

Hollie laughed. "And did he except the invitation?"

"Like a true gentleman he accepted and turned up the following night."

"Oh my God!" Hollie said with her hand over her mouth. "I so wish I could have been there."

Beth was laughing so much that she struggled to get out all the words.

"He showed up with flowers for my mum. Not for me! Spent most of the evening talking to my dad about rowing and cricket. We did manage to go for a short walk, just the two of us. He's so gorgeous."

"I'm pleased for you, Beth. When are you seeing him again?"

"Tonight – he's picking me up and taking me to the cinema."

Hollie smiled, pleased that her best friend had found someone decent at last.

"And you? Did Samson get you home alright? You were a bit trollied. I've not seen you drink like that for years."

The waitress placed their coffees on the table.

"Yes, he got me home alright. The following day he took me to the seaside. It was lovely. We had fish and chips on the beach. While we were there, we bumped into an old friend of Samson's who had moved there with his girlfriend."

Beth took a sip of her coffee, eager to hear more of the story.

"When we saw him again later, as we were leaving, he was being attacked by a group of men. So, Samson went to help."

Beth looked worried. "Oh no! Is Samson alright?"

"Yes, he's fine. He fought them off – one of them actually held a knife to my throat!"

"No!" Beth said, a look of horror on her face. "I can't believe it! Are you both alright?"

"Yes, we're fine. Samson only has a bruise and a cut on his face."

"Bloody hell, Hollie, you certainly live life in the fast lane! How are things between you both now?"

Hollie took a sip off her coffee, then pushed it to one side.

"He's so gentle, but tough. So kind but quite complex. I don't think he thinks that he's good in relationships, but he's always trying to make me happy."

"Oh, Hollie, at last. Do you think you've found the one?"

"I don't know, Beth; I've only known him a short while. I thought Marcus was the man for me and look how wrong I was there. Let's wait and see."

Beth finished her coffee.

"Shall we go shopping? I can't wait to choose a new dress for this wedding. I might even take Peter with me." Beth stood up. "Aren't you drinking yours?"

"No, I haven't felt great since that night out. Maybe too much alcohol and my body is still recovering. I just need a couple of days to let my stomach settle."

The girls left the coffee shop, walking up the high street towards their favourite clothes shop. Hollie took a deep sigh as they walked in. She knew that Beth would take some time choosing an outfit. Beth adored fashion, she loved experimenting and trying new combinations. Hollie grabbed a few items off the rails, sticking to her familiar favourites. Beth had already gathered up quite a selection of clothes which she draped over her arm. When she could carry no more, she turned round to Hollie.

"Shall we go try this lot on? Even though I don't think I can afford half of the clothes I've chosen."

Hollie followed her into the changing room, sitting down in one of the armchairs placed near the entrance.

"You go ahead, take your time. I'm going to sit right here." She smiled at her friend, sitting back in the armchair. Beth disappeared into the cubicle, trying on the outfits one by one, coming out for a little spin and a catwalk turn each time.

"I think this one is my favourite," she said, stepping out in a short puffy candyfloss pink dress and parading up and down.

"You look fabulous in that."

Beth paid for the dress, pleased that she had found an outfit that she loved.

"I need to buy some shoes to match now."

The girls walked further up the high street, looking in every shoe shop they passed.

"Look at them," Beth said as they stopped in front of an elegant shoe shop, pointing to a pair of pink and white polka dot platform shoes.

"Let's go in so I can try them on." She took hold of Hollie's arm, pulling her into the shoe shop and asked the assistant to fetch them from the window display.

"A perfect fit!" Beth said as she stood up, marvelling at her shoes. "What do you think, Hollie?"

"Yes, they're certainly you! They'll look fabulous with your dress."

Beth slid them off, handing them to the shop assistant.

"Can you put these in a box, please? I'll take them."

She was so pleased she had the perfect outfit. As they left the shop, Beth spotted a new accessory shop across the road.

"Shall we go have a look in there? I might get a nice hat to match my dress."

Hollie suddenly stopped walking and caught Beth's arm.

"I think I need to sit down; I feel quite faint."

"Oh no, Hollie." She grabbed her arm tightly. "Can you make it to that bench?"

Beth supported her, walking her slowly to the nearby bench where Hollie sat for a moment, taking in some deep breaths, relieved to be sitting down. She closed her eyes for a few seconds. Beth sat beside her, placing her hand behind her just in case she fainted and toppled backwards.

"I'm sorry, Beth, I'll be alright in a minute or two. I just need to be still for a bit."

Beth was concerned for her friend.

"Maybe your blood pressure is high or something. You really should make a doctor's appointment."

Hollie's doctor was back home in Cornwall; she hadn't had a reason to visit a doctor while she had been up here in the city.

"Please don't worry, it's nothing. I'll be fine after I've had a rest. I just think I'm tired – I've had a lot of late nights recently."

They sat for a while, watching shoppers hurry past, then Hollie turned to Beth.

"I think I'm alright now."

Beth looked at her, not convinced.

"I'm not sure, Hollie; you still look a little pale. There's a chemist across the street; let's go over and see what the pharmacist thinks."

Hollie was reluctant but could see how worried Beth was and could see little point in refusing. She stood up, feeling less lightheaded now. Beth linked her arm and led her slowly across the road. A mature, pleasant-looking lady, clearly the pharmacist, greeted them from behind the counter.

"Hello girls, what can I get for you?"

Beth smiled, deciding immediately that she would do the talking so that Hollie wouldn't play down any of her symptoms.

"My friend has been feeling a little faint recently and not quite herself."

The pharmacist came out from behind the counter, stepping closer to Hollie.

"What other symptoms do you have? Are you eating and drinking normally?"

"Now you mention it, I don't seem to have much of an appetite. I often feel a bit queasy and I'm so tired."

Reaching up for a small box behind the counter, the pharmacist then passed it to Hollie.

"Try this. If I'm wrong, then make a doctor's appointment as it might be diabetes or a blood pressure issue."

Hollie looked at the writing on the outside of the box.

"Sorry," she said, holding out the box to pass back. "I think you've picked up the wrong thing – this is a pregnancy test."

"Yes, I know. I'd eliminate that first."

Hollie stood for a moment with her arm stretched out, waiting for her to take back the box, thinking she was crazy.

Beth stepped forward and paid.

"Thank you," she said and took Hollie's arm once again, leading her out of the shop.

"Why did you buy a pregnancy test? I'm not pregnant," said Hollie, relieved to be out in the fresh air.

"I'm sure you're not Hollie, but like the lady said, eliminate that, then you can make an appointment to see a doctor. Maybe you're just lacking in something."

Hollie looked worried. "I'm always so careful. It would be my worst nightmare to be pregnant now, right in the middle of my studies. My entire life's dreams and ambitions are to become a vet. I'm so close to it now. Nothing can stop me. I *know* I can't be pregnant. What a ridiculous idea!"

"Are you sure you've been careful with Samson?"

"You're sounding like my mother – of course I've been careful," replied Hollie impatiently. "I'm always careful."

They crossed back over to the other side of the street, joining the queue at the bus-stop.

"Do you want me to come back with you?" Beth said, placing her shopping bags on the ground to give her arms a rest as Hollie, who was feeling pretty exhausted, rubbed her forehead.

"Thanks, Beth, but I'll be fine. I'll probably have a lie down. Samson will be back later – he said he would cook tea."

"Ah, that's so sweet of him. I'm so glad you found him. There's something about the two of you which makes me think you belong together."

Hollie laughed.

"Oh, shut up Beth, you're a romantic fool. I'm the cynical one; nobody knows how long they will stay with someone for. Do you believe Peter is your man?

Is he truly your happy ever after?"

Beth looked at her with dreamy eyes. "Yeah, I think he is."

The bus appeared and pulled up beside them, its smelly fumes wafting down the queue as, one by one, the passengers boarded. The girls found a seat together on the top deck, looking out over the busy streets. They chatted for the entire journey home, planning more shopping days and nights out. Both were looking forward to starting their last year of university, determined to take full advantage of their last months as students before their lives took a new path.

Hollie stood up and pressed the buzzer.

"Are you sure that you don't want me to walk back with you?" Beth said, smiling at her friend.

"Honestly, I'll be fine. I'll call you later." Hollie leant down to Beth, giving her a peck on the cheek. "Talk soon."

She walked carefully down the steps, thanking the driver as she stepped onto the pavement. The walk back wasn't far, just the length of Stanley Street. The sun was shining, surrounded by pure blue skies. Hollie felt warm. After walking up the stairs to the apartment in the heat, she headed straight to the kitchen where she poured herself a large glass of cold water.

In the front room, she sank onto the settee and was tempted to fall asleep, even though it was just after lunchtime. Maybe she was diabetic. She decided to concertedly eat better and would make an appointment at the family doctor's when she returned home, possibly next week when Samson had finished the work on the apartment.

She got up to make herself a sandwich. Leaving it on the side, she headed to the bathroom, an image of the crazy pharmacist in the chemist appearing in her head. Maybe Beth was right; ruling out this absurd possibility would enable her own doctor to look for anything else that might be wrong.

Following the instructions, she left the pregnancy test on the side of the bath while she went to eat her sandwich. The instructions had said to leave for two minutes, but it was more like twenty by the time she remembered to go back to it. She had left the box next to it so she could put the stick back into the box and put the whole stupid thing straight into the bin.

She picked up the stick. The blue line indicated that the test was complete; the red line indicated that she was pregnant. Deciding to read the instructions again, she wondered if maybe the red line indicated a negative result and she had carelessly got it mixed up. Her legs felt wobbly, then a feeling of nausea swept over her. She sat down on the side of the bath. *This must be wrong!* In a small box, the words 'six weeks' appeared in blue writing. She slid off the side of the bath onto the floor, clutching the stick. Her heart beat so loudly she thought that anyone could have heard it. Leaning over the toilet, she felt that she might be sick. She closed her eyes, taking long deep breaths, trying to take control of her body. In and out, she took slow, deep breaths. *How could this be?* She vomited into the toilet. How could her life be ruined this way? She sat on the bathroom floor as tears ran down her cheeks.

After a few minutes, she stood up, placing the stick back into the box. She went into the bedroom and sat down on the bed. Never had she felt so sad and alone. Looking around at Samson's apartment, she wondered why he would want her once he knew that she was pregnant with another man's child. She couldn't tell him. How would she say goodbye? Taking another deep breath, she picked up the phone, wiped her eyes and rang her mother.

"Hello Hollie, how lovely to hear from you!"

Hollie tried to compose herself.

"Hello, Mum. I know this is short notice but I'm coming home tonight. Can you tell Dad I'll text him later when I know what train I'll arrive on so he can pick me up from the station?"

"Oh Hollie, of course! That's wonderful! Is everything alright?"

"Yes, Mum, everything's fine. I must go, I've a lot to do. I'll see you later tonight," she said, her voice starting to tremble. Tears poured from her eyes after hearing her mum's voice and she wished she could be home now, longing for her mum to wrap her arms around her, telling her everything would be alright.

She opened the wardrobe and took out her holdall. She packed all her belongings, zipped it shut, then placed it beside the front door. In the lounge, she sat down and rang a taxi to pick her up in fifteen minutes to take her to the station. Next, she placed a plain piece of paper in front of her, wondering how she to explain to Samson why she had to go. Picking up the pen, she began to write.

Dear Samson, she began, barely holding back the tears just writing his name. This past week had been like living someone else's life; now it was time to return to hers. She didn't want him to feel sorry for her, trying to help her in some way, showing his pity, offering his help by providing a life for her and her child. He mustn't know the truth. She began to write, unsure of how to say goodbye. Taking a deep breath, she focused, thinking of only one thing: to get on that train, go home and spend some time with her mum and dad. Beyond that, she didn't know.

She left the note on the coffee table, locked the front door and pushed the key back through the letter box. The taxi picked her up outside, taking her directly to the station.

On the platform, her train to Cornwall was waiting. She found a window seat, placed her bag in the rack above and sat back in her seat. The doors banged shut, followed by the guard's whistle and then the train pulled out of the station. That was the moment that she felt her heart breaking: for the first time, she knew what Samson meant to her, yet she knew that now they couldn't have a future together and she must let him go.

Picking up her phone, she messaged her dad to collect her from the station. Her future was uncertain now. She had worked so hard these past three years, studying for her veterinary degree, and, as she prepared to go into her last year, she knew she was on course to finish with top grades. Having a baby on her own, just a few weeks before her final exams, wasn't a realistic option that she could think about right now. Maybe, she thought, staying at home in Cornwall was the more sensible option. One thing she truly knew was that no matter what, Marcus must never know he was the father of her child.

As she looked out of the window, the train picked up speed, whizzing past streets, and row and upon row of houses. Soon, the city had been left behind, replaced by fields and countryside dotted with farmhouses and villages. She took out her phone again. First, she messaged Bob, explaining that she needed to take two weeks off, then she messaged Beth, apologising for texting and explaining that she couldn't talk right now. She also told her about the test showing a positive result and that it stated six weeks. At the end of the text, she said she was returning home for now and would ring in a couple of days.

She glanced at her watch. Samson would be getting home soon. She imagined for a moment how their evening would have been spent together: she pictured him walking in through the door with a bag of clothes, planning to move in with her for a while, but then she forced her mind away from such thoughts and wearily closed her eyes.

Chapter Twelve

Samson unlocked the apartment door, pushing it open with his foot. As he placed his bag down in the hallway, he caught sight of the apartment key card that he had given to Hollie. He picked it up, thinking maybe she had dropped it earlier. He headed to the kitchen, clutching a casserole dish that he had just collected from his mum's house, which he carefully placed on a shelf in the fridge.

"Hollie?" he called out. "Are you here?" The silence in the apartment indicated to him that Hollie was still out, still shopping with Beth. He glanced at his phone – no missed calls from her. He took a bottle of beer from the fridge and went into the lounge where he took a long drink standing in front of the window. As he looked out over the balcony, the sun set lower in the sky, almost disappearing behind the buildings in the distance. He sat on the settee, his feet on the coffee table, and leaned back, relaxing for a moment after his busy day. As he placed his empty bottle on the table, he caught sight of a folded piece of paper with his name on. He paused, not wanting to pick it up: surely it couldn't be a goodbye note from Hollie? everything had been fine this morning – but why wasn't she there? He reached forward and picked it up.

Dear Samson, meeting you was one of the best things that has happened to me in a very long time. You came into my life when things weren't good and showed me that it could be fun again, with the right person to share it with. I know now that I'm not the right girl for you. We are very different, and both lead quite different lives.

Please know that I have loved spending time with you these past few days, but now we must go our separate ways. I wish you good luck in your business with Hector and hope that one day you'll settle with the right girl. Please don't try to contact me.

Hollie x

He folded the note, placing it back on the table. Brushing his hands over his head, he closed his eyes. He certainly hadn't seen this coming. He took out his phone and rang Hollie's number. It rang continuously – *had she blocked his calls?*

Standing up, he walked over to the balcony doors and looked across the city. Where could she have gone? Why did she not think they were right for each other? Surely she had felt what he felt?

The door buzzer interrupted his unanswered questions. He hurried down the hallway, part of him thinking it might be Hollie, coming back to talk to him.

He swung the door open.

"Oh, hello Sophia, sorry – I forgot you were calling by."

Leaving the door open for her to let herself in, he was already halfway back up the hallway to the lounge.

"You look like you've had some bad news; is everything alright?" Sophia said as she shut the door. In the lounge, she sat beside him; he handed her the note.

"She's gone."

Sophia started to read, looking up at Samson halfway through. When she had finished, she placed it back on the coffee table.

"Oh Samson, I'm so sorry. I know you really liked her. What happened? Did you argue over something?"

"I don't know. I left her this morning, and everything was fine. She told me to bring some clothes back with me so I could stay here with her for a while."

"You must have done or said something." Sophia pushed his leg, trying to get him to tell her.

"No, we didn't argue. I could never argue with her. I just need to look at her and I back down immediately."

"I wish you would do that to me," Sophia replied. "Have you tried ringing her?"

"Yes, but she must have blocked my number. Like she says, she doesn't think we are right for each other. I can't change the way she feels. I don't want to hound her like her ex-boyfriend. It's over; I just have to accept it."

"It doesn't make any sense. The way that she looks at you... It doesn't feel right. Don't you think she's worth fighting for, but not with your fists this time? You have to find her."

"I hardly know anything about her. I have no idea where she might have gone."

Sophia paused for a moment. "Why don't you ring the restaurant? They'll know; maybe they'll tell you where she's gone."

She didn't give him chance to reply; she took out her phone and rang the number for the restaurant. A man with a foreign accent answered.

"Good evening, BB's restaurant, how may I help you?"

Sophia's voice changed in tone to that of a sweet, polite young lady.

"Good evening. I'm so sorry to bother you, you must be so busy, but I was hoping you might be able to help me find my friend Hollie. Could you tell me where I can find her please?"

The voice on the other line paused.

"May I ask who's calling, please?"

"It's Sophia, Samson's sister." She waited, thinking she had probably blown it now – if Hollie didn't want to see her brother again, she had probably left instructions with work not to tell him anything. The line went quiet for a moment, then the voice came back on the line.

"Hello there. Yes, Hollie's gone back home to Cornwall for a couple of weeks. I don't have her parents' phone number, but I do have Beth's – her best friend. She'll know how to get in touch with her."

Sophia grabbed a pen, taking down the number as he called it out.

"Thank you, you have been most helpful."

She put her phone back into her pocket and pushed the piece of paper with Beth's number on it across the table to Samson.

"Ring Beth. She knows where she is."

Samson was still reluctant to chase her.

"Why would she tell me anything? She's Hollie's best friend and Hollie would have told her that she doesn't want to see me. It's a waste of time."

Sophia got up.

"Well, I'm off to Mum's for tea. Are you going to feel sorry for yourself or do you want to come with me?"

"No thanks, I think I'll stay here for a bit. I'll catch up with you later."

Sophia gave him a kiss on the cheek.

"Ring Beth. If you don't want to let her go, then you need to do something."

She closed the door, leaving Samson alone in silence. He switched on the television, thinking he might watch some sport. Then he picked up his phone, scrolling through his friends, trying to decide who he might call to arrange a night out with the boys. But it was no good; he didn't want to do either of those things. He placed his phone on the coffee table. That morning, he remembered holding and kissing her before he left. To think now that that was their goodbye. He pictured her sitting up in bed, her beautiful face, her messed-up hair falling over her shoulders, smiling at him. *What could have happened?*

Eventually, he reached forward, picked up his phone and dialled Beth's number. It rang several times and, with each ring, he started to doubt that this was a good idea and was on the verge of hanging up when he heard a familiar voice

"Hello?" Beth said.

He waited for a moment; he knew Beth was his only chance of finding Hollie.

"Hello Beth, it's Samson."

There was a long silence, but he knew she hadn't hung up.

"Samson? As in Hollie's Samson?"

"Yes, but I don't think I'm Hollie's Samson anymore. She's gone – but I guess you know that. I don't want to harass her; I just want to see her. Do you know where she is?"

"Samson, please, I don't think it's my place to tell you. I'll tell her that you were asking after her when I talk to her next. I'm sorry too – you were probably the best man she has ever been out with and she was certainly falling for you. Look, I've probably said too much already. I'll tell her you rang."

"Wait, please don't hang up just yet, please hear me out. I've never met anyone like Hollie before; she captivated my heart from the moment I saw her. She didn't give me a second glance to start with but the more I saw her and got to know her, the more I began to fall in love with her and there wasn't anything I wouldn't do for her. Please, Beth, tell me why she left and I'll try to fix it! Help me win her heart back. Whatever I've done, I'll put it right."

Beth took a big sigh. She knew that he cared about Hollie more than she knew.

"Samson, you can't fix this." She paused. "Hollie found out today that she is pregnant with Marcus's baby. She knew that she had to let you go. There – I've said it."

Samson was silent.

"See, just as she thought: you don't want her now."

He shut his eyes. What must she be going through? He broke the silence between them.

"Where is she? Please tell me she's not facing this alone?"

Beth could tell from his voice that his only concern was for Hollie, not for what she had just told him and how it might affect him; Hollie was his priority and who was taking care of her. Her heart began to melt with sadness for him, and for Hollie too. He really did love her.

"She'll probably never speak to me again, but she's gone to her parents in Cornwall. Get a pen and I'll give you the address."

Samson took down the address.

"Thank you, Beth." His voice was trembling at being given a chance to see Hollie one more time.

He grabbed his coat and put on his shoes.

"What must she be going through?" He knew how important this last university year was to her, and her dreams to become a vet. Wherever she was tonight, he knew she would be scared, upset and feeling alone. He knew he had to find her. Closing the apartment door behind him, he hurried down the stairs, out into the street and got into his truck.

*

In the dark, the train slowly pulled into Penzance Station. It was the end of the line and the train emptied out. People rushed to gather their belongings, quickly getting of the train and hurrying up the platform. Hollie picked up her holdall; she was one of the last to step on to the platform. Standing still, she inhaled the familiar smell of the sea. As the crowds began to disperse, she looked down the platform towards the ticket office and station building. Dressed in green trousers and an old grey jumper, a man stood with both hands in his pockets looking up the platform towards her. Hollie smiled, remembering that her dad had no fashion sense. She hurried towards him, clutching her bag. Before she'd reached him, tears were rolling down her face. Sure that they were happy tears, she threw her arms around him. Lifting her from the ground, her dad gave her the embrace that she had needed.

"Hey girl, it's not like you to give your old dad such a hug. Have you missed us then?"

"Dad – it's good to be home."

He picked up her bag with one hand, placing the other around her shoulder.

"The car's outside; let's get you home. You must have a lot of news to tell us."

He unlocked the car, placing her bag on the back seat.

"Don't tell your mother, but I was pleased you ditched that Marcus. I never was struck on the chap from when you first brought him home to meet us."

Hollie smiled at him. He started the engine and drove out of the station car park and onto the main road. She was pleased that soon she would be home.

"Is there someone else?"

"Not really, Dad." Hollie looked away from him, staring out of the window, not wanting to answer any questions right now.

He smiled at his daughter.

"I'm not sure I believe you, young lady, but I think you'll talk to me when you're ready."

Hollie looked across at him and smiled. She knew he could tell that she was hiding the truth but right now she wasn't ready to tell him anything. She hadn't fully accepted herself what was about to happen in her life, so for now she knew he would wait.

"How's Mum?"

Her dad laughed.

"You know your mother; how do you think? You give her a few hours' notice that you're coming home and you might as well throw a grenade into the house. This afternoon she's been making cakes, preparing your room and making your favourite tea."

Hollie's eyes widened with anticipation.

"Please tell me she's been making pasties for supper?"

He returned her question with a simple smile.

"Oh, yes!" Hollie said. "I'm *starving*."

The car turned off the main road, driving up a narrow lane for several miles. He drove slowly as the road twisted down a steep hill. Halfway down, turning left along a single track, Hollie knew that from here she could see across the bay and out into the Atlantic Ocean. They pulled off the track and slowly drove up a stony driveway which opened out onto a large area in front of the house. The large cottage-style detached house stood behind a small stone wall and every window was lit up.

"I'm assuming that both of my sisters are at home."

"Fay hasn't long been back. She started work at her new job in Truro last week – she's not enjoying the commute each day, but I'm sure she'll get used to it."

Hollie opened the car door, stepping out onto the gravel drive.

"I'm so pleased for her; she's worked hard for that bank in Penzance for years – she certainly deserved her promotion. How about my lazy sister, what she's she been up to?"

Her dad opened the back passenger door, taking out her holdall.

"Heather…" He paused for a moment while he walked round the car to Hollie. "Heather has moved Ray into her bedroom. They're saving for a deposit, and they tell me that they don't want to waste money renting."

Hollie looked at him, both award that neither of her sisters were keen on leaving home any time soon. She opened the small iron gate then, taking her bag from her dad, she walked up the path to the porch where she stopped and turned around. From here, she knew she would at last see one of her favourite views. Her dad closed the gate and walked up the path towards her. In the distance, she could see the little harbour, the houses with lights dotted from the bay up the hillside, the moon offering just enough light to see the gentle movement of the water.

"Come on, let's get you in."

Hollie pushed the front door open and walked into the hallway. Her mum must have heard the car.

"My daring Hollie!" She flung her arms around her, hugging her for a few moments. "It's been too long; oh, I've missed you."

"I've missed you too, Mum."

Hollie followed her down the hallway to the kitchen, from where a beautiful smell was coming.

"Come and sit down, you must be hungry after such a long journey."

Hollie sat down at the large table. The fire was lit and gave off a warm glow. Her mum placed a plate with a large warm pasty and baked beans in front of her and Hollie tucked in, pleased to be home.

Her sister Fay walked into the kitchen after hearing voices.

"Hey Hollie, what a nice surprise! Mum told me you were coming home tonight."

Hollie smiled, pleased to see her older sister. "How are you getting on in your new job?"

Fay sat down beside her. "I'm really enjoying it; I'm so lucky to have this opportunity. Just need to get used to the hour and a half journey each way. How's university?"

Hollie continued eating her supper. "It's all going good, thanks, Fay."

"Is everything alright, Hollie?" asked her mother who had joined them. "I got the feeling that you were upset when you rang me earlier."

Her dad put her bag down beside her.

"Let her eat, she's had a long journey."

Hollie looked at her mum.

"This is delicious, Mum, the best meal I've had in ages." Then she paused, and looked up again at her clearly worried mum. "Everything's fine, really."

She just wanted to get through each day as it came. Getting home was the first step, then she would take the next few days to decided what to do next. Tonight, she was tired, so maybe tomorrow she would talk properly to her mum and dad.

"Where are Heather and Ray?"

Hollie's mum raised both eyebrows.

"They're upstairs, watching a movie, treating this as a youth hostel. They only come down to eat and drink."

Hollie glanced briefly at her dad. He smiled, not wanting to give his opinion; he obviously didn't want to take sides, but certainly he didn't want to disagree with Hollie's mum.

"I can't believe you ended things with that nice boy, Marcus." Her mum was still fishing for details.

Hollie didn't want to talk about this tonight.

"Mum, do you mind if we talk about that another time? He turned out not so nice after all."

Hollie's dad poured himself a fresh cup of tea from the pot.

"Shall I pour one for you, Hollie?"

"Yes, please, Dad. I think I'll take it up to bed with me." She picked up her bag and gave both her mum and dad a kiss on the cheek. "It's so nice to be home."

Hollie closed her bedroom door, dropping her bag on her bed as she walked over to the window. Her room was at the front of the house, overlooking the driveway and the bay. She closed the curtains then, sitting on the bed, began to unpack her bag. As she took out her jeans, Samson's white T-shirt fell out. She held it against her face, his smell making her close her eyes, imagining him there with her, knowing she was needlessly torturing herself. She opened her eyes; he was gone from her life now, there was no going back from this. She folded the top neatly and placed it back in her bag.

She changed and got into bed, sipping her tea. After a few minutes, she switched off her bedside lamp, and lay back on the pillow.

Home at last, surrounded by the people who loved her dearly; but tonight she felt alone. Despite the fact that her heart was beating, she knew it was broken. In the darkness, she turned to face the window, her pillow soaking up the tears that fell from her face.

Chapter Thirteen

It could have been the strong winds, gusting on to the side of the house, or the pounding rain beating against the window that woke her early the next morning. Hollie opened her eyes and looked across at the small pink, child's clock that sat on her dresser. It was 8 o'clock and the house was quiet; then she remembered it was Sunday.

She threw back her covers and walked over to open the curtains. The previous evening had been dark when she had arrived and now she desperately needed to be reminded of the dramatic view from her bedroom window. As a small child, it had meant nothing to her, but in her late teens, and now in her twenties, she found it captivating. She stood still for a moment.

"No," she thought, shaking her head and staring into the distance. "Nothing has changed."

Rougher now than it had been last night, the sea was crashing over the rocks at the bottom of the cliff, the waves repeatedly hammering the land. She knew that the tide was in as it came up high against the harbour wall. The fishing boats, moored up within the harbour wall, bobbed up and down.

Despite the stormy weather, Hollie desperately wanted to get out in the fresh air. She knew that the village would soon be busy and the fisherman would soon be tending to their boats; a day not spent at sea often meant a day of maintenance. The village shop was a community hub where many would pass the time of day. She quickly put on some warm clothes and a hat (mainly to hide her messy morning hair) then, as quietly as she could, went downstairs to find her welly boots and rain mac.

Outside, it was raining, and the wind was blowing ferociously. She was forced to walk slowly against the wind, down the road towards the harbour. She held onto the corners of her hood so as not to let the wind in. As she got closer to the harbour and further down into the bay, the wind began to calm down. Seagulls squawked noisily overhead, looking for scraps. Conditions were too treacherous for the fishermen today. She crossed the road to the convenience shop and went in to get out of the cold. A mature woman wearing a multi-coloured cardigan and fingerless gloves immediately recognised her.

"Hollie, what a lovely surprise," she said, getting up and opening the hatch.

"Let me have a proper look at you, my girl," she said, putting her arms around her and giving her a gentle hug.

"Hello, Mrs Goodberry, it's so good to see you too! How's business?"

Hollie naturally gave Mrs Goodberry a big smile; she had known her all her life. Mr and Mrs Goodberry had owned the shop since she had been a baby.

"Business is going well, my dear, although I'm trying to convince Mr Goodberry that we should sell up and retire, but he won't hear of it." She returned to her place behind the counter and sat back on her stool. "You must come over for tea and cakes one afternoon while you're home."

Hollie picked up a newspaper for her dad and some chocolate for them both to share later when her mum was cooking lunch.

"I'd love to, Mrs Goodberry – maybe we could work on Mr Goodberry together."

Hollie knew that her husband was a delightful man and that it wouldn't take too much for Mrs Goodberry to persuade him to sell up. She was sure that he was already planning their retirement now that he knew his wife wanted to retire.

"You know, I'd love to hear about everything you've been up to in the city. You're such a clever girl, going to university – your parents are so proud of you."

Hollie handed her the money for the paper and chocolate.

"Thanks, Mrs Goodberry. I'll take you up on that offer one afternoon. You know I can't resist your lovely cakes."

She folded the paper, placing it inside her raincoat, then went outside to be greeted by the persistent rain. Crossing the road, she started walking alongside the harbour, watching the choppy swell swirling and crashing against the wall. Feeling a hand on her shoulder, she turned around to be greeted by a friendly smile.

"You be careful walking so close to that wall on such a windy day," said a young man. Then he paused, staring at her a moment. "Is it Hollie?"

"Jim?" Hollie said, his face now becoming clearer to her. "We went to primary school together, didn't we?" She remembered him as a sporty boy, never paying attention in lessons, just wanting to get out on that football field.

"I heard that you'd gone to university. You've done so well. Are you visiting your family?"

She took down her hood, stepping slightly away from the wall.

"Yes, probably just a couple of weeks, I'm not sure yet."

Jim smiled. "Maybe if you are free one evening, I can take you for a drink?" He paused, waiting for a reply; it wasn't often he bumped into such a pretty girl, and taking advantage of the fact they had known one another as children was a hopeful start.

Hollie smiled. She couldn't believe that she was being asked out by a chap who wasn't bad-looking on a rainy Sunday morning.

"That sounds lovely, Jim, but I don't think I'll be here very long." She wanted to tell him that her heart belonged to one man, a man who she would never see again; that no other man could ever take his place; and that right now she couldn't possibly imagine going out with anyone else.

"It is so good to see you again, Jim. You take care."

She smiled and pulled her hood back over her head, then began to walk back up the road towards home. The rain was lashing down now, and she tried to walk quickly but going uphill with the wind head-on was a continuous test. She walked in through the front door, leaving her wellies and mac to dry in the porch.

In the kitchen, the fire had already been lit, and her dad was drinking tea and eating toast while her mum stood peeling vegetables.

"Have you been out in this?" her mum asked, not quite believing that one of her daughters could get out of bed before her on a Sunday morning.

"I just needed a bit of fresh air – you can't beat a morning walk to kick-start the day." She still felt damp but didn't want to admit that maybe she should have waited till the stormy weather had passed.

"You go and put some warm clothes on and I'll bring you up a nice cup of coffee," said her mum.

Hollie gave her dad the newspaper, a little soggy round the edges.

"Do you mind if I have tea, Mum? I've gone off coffee recently."

Her dad winked at her, acknowledging his appreciation of the newspaper she'd brought for him. Keen to get some dry clothes on, Hollie went back upstairs where she found an old hoodie and some jeans. Closing her eyes briefly, she sat up on her bed with her legs crossed in front of her, finally feeling warm and dry. She loved being home, it was a comfortable, safe feeling. But, for the first time, she felt that she didn't quite belong here anymore. This was her past, not her future. Her thoughts were interrupted by a knock at her bedroom door and her mum walked in. First, she placed some clothes on her dressing table, then a cup of tea beside her bed. She sat down on the end of the bed.

"I'm worried about you, Hollie – is everything alright? You know if you want to talk to me about anything, I'm always here."

Hollie desperately wanted to talk to her, but she knew she wasn't ready yet. She had to figure out everything in her own head first. How could she tell her mum that she was going to drop out of her degree and, to top it off, that she would have to move back home to have a baby that she couldn't support?

"I'm alright, Mum, I've just had a crazy couple of weeks and I need to step back for a bit. Can we talk about things in a couple of days?" she said and smiled at her mum.

"Yes, of course, my dear."

Her mum stood up and caught sight of someone driving towards to house. She stepped closer to the window to see if she might recognise the car.

"Looks like another visitor coming to see Fay again."

Hollie heard the car slowing down outside on the driveway. The noise on the gravelly stones gave away the sort of vehicle Fay's visitor was driving. As a girl, Hollie had got used to hearing vehicles come and go, reversing backwards and forwards; she knew Fay's visitor had a big vehicle.

She took a big sip of her tea.

"Ooh, he looks rather handsome; I don't think I've seen him before."

Hollie lay back on her pillow, not interested in her mum's nosiness about Fay's boyfriends. Her mum was still peering outside from behind the curtains.

"Mum, come away from the window, he might see you."

"He must be rather keen to visit her on a Sunday morning. I don't know if she's even up yet. Shame he's come out in such awful weather in that big white truck when Fay's probably still asleep."

Hollie was off the bed and at the window like a bullet out of a gun. She pulled back the curtain, looking down at the driveway. Samson's truck was parked outside, and he was walking towards the house.

Her heart now racing, questions rushing through her mind. *Why is he here? How did he find me?*

"Mum, please get rid of him."

"Who is he?"

"Mum, there's no time, please. I can't see him – please tell him I'm not here."

Her voice began to tremble and tears were welling up in her eyes. Her mum looked confused but nonetheless, she came away from the window.

"Don't worry, dear, I'll get rid of him." She left, closing the bedroom door behind her.

Hollie stood next to the window, waiting to see Samson walk back to his truck.

There was a loud, firm knock at the front door. Hollie's mum opened the door to a young good-looking man standing in the rain.

"Hello, sorry to bother you so early on a Sunday morning, but I'm not sure I'm at the right house. I'm looking for Hollie?"

She looked at him for a moment. He seemed polite and there was something sincere about the way he asked for Hollie, the anticipation in his eyes, his desperation to see her.

"I'm sorry, she isn't here."

Samson's face dropped; he had driven most of the night in shocking weather to get here. The thought of seeing Hollie, if only for a few minutes, had been the only thing that had kept him going. He stepped back from the porch.

"I'm sorry to have bothered you," he said and began to walk back to his truck.

Hollie's dad appeared at the front door.

"Are you Samson?"

Samson stopped, turning around to the man standing in the porchway.

"Yes, indeed – I'm Samson."

Her dad stood to one side.

"You best come in, then."

Hollie's mum stared frantically at her husband as Samson stepped into the porch.

"Give me your coat, young man."

Samson didn't know what to say, he just stood there like a lost little boy.

Her dad smiled, trying to put him at ease.

"I took a phone call this morning, while Hollie was out walking, from her best friend Beth."

He took Samson's coat, hanging it next to Hollie's.

"Beth told me that you would be coming down; she also told me the sort of man you are and what Hollie means to you."

"Thank you. I just wanted to see her, even for a few minutes."

"Go on up. Her room is at the end of the landing."

Samson took a deep breath and went up the stairs and along the landing until he reached the last door. He knocked gently.

Hollie still stood peering out of the widow, waiting to watch Samson walk away. She froze at the sound of the knock.

"Hollie, please forgive me for coming to your home. I just wanted to make sure you're alright, then I promise I'll go and leave you in peace."

She closed her eyes. Hearing his voice again, her strong feelings for him came flooding back. She couldn't breathe and her heart pounded. She couldn't tell him the truth; they couldn't be together, not now. She went to the door.

"Please leave, Samson, we don't have anything to talk about."

Samson put the palm of his hand against the door.

"I know," he said, and paused. "Beth told me."

She stepped away from the door. "I don't understand – why are you here then?"

"The night I carried you out of Marcus's apartment, I carried you both out. From that night, I fell in love with you, not bearing to spend a single day without hearing your voice, seeing your beautiful face and catching hold of your hand. I can't imagine my life without you in it. Open the door and tell me you don't love me too and I'll walk away. Then I'll leave you with my heart forever."

Hollie placed the palm of her hand on the back of

the door, tears running down her cheeks, knowing he was close. She could bear it no more and opened the door, seeing the man she adored, the man she truly loved.

"But I'm carrying another man's child. How can you love me now?"

Samson stepped closer to her, wiping her tears from her face with his hand.

"It's your child, growing in you. I love you, Hollie, and I'll love your child. It might not be mine, but I'll love it as if it were. Being a good dad is not about being there at the conception; it's about loving and protecting that child. Let me love you both. I feel empty without you; I've never felt like this before. If you want to stay here in Cornwall, I'll move down here We can rent a small house in the village. Or, if you want to finish your degree, we can live in the city. I'll look after you, and when the baby arrives, I'll care for you both while you take your final exams. Wherever you want to be in this world, I want to be with you."

Hollie had thought that she had lost him for good, her heart broken since she'd walked away from him. But now he was stood in front of her and her heart was racing.

Samson reached forward, touching her face, his eyes focused on her eyes.

"Please don't cry."

"I feel such a fool; I've been so stupid." She looked away from him. "I've ruined what we could have had."

He placed both his hands on her face, moving closer to her.

"No, don't say that. We still have it. What we have is special. I've never met anyone like you before. I'd never fallen in love with anyone till I met you. You've shown me what it feels like to love someone with all your heart and to never want to be without them. Please give me a chance." He leaned closer towards her.

"Tell me you don't love me."

She put her hands on his chest.

"I knew when you picked me up and carried me out that night, I knew then I would fall in love with you. You captivated me and my heart, and I couldn't help but fall more and more in love with you. I didn't know if my heart would be strong enough to let you go."

He kissed her, picking her up in his arms, spinning her around with happiness, before gently putting her back down. Wrapping his arms around her, he held her close to his chest, then closed his eyes for a moment, relieved that he had got his girl back.

Hollie wiped her tears from her face, looked at him and smiled.

"Come on, I'd better introduce you to my family. Then, if the rain has stopped, perhaps I can show you around the village."

He took hold of her hand as she led him downstairs to meet her parents.

The rain had now stopped and the grey clouds slightly parted, allowing a tiny glimpse of the sun to sneak through and shine on the bay. Samson and Hollie walked down the road towards the harbour, hands entwined, enjoying the moment of planning their lives together.

The End